Second Printing, 2017

ISBN 10: 0692893563

ISBN 13: 978-0-692-89356-2

The Journey Home

Home

Matthew Miller

Dedicated to all those who believed in me for completing this feat. Especially to my parents for teaching me about the values of history.

Chapter I

Decisions Come from the Heart

The sky was clear with no clouds for miles, the sun shining down on the beautiful farmland and glistening off the bright reds and yellows of the fall leaves. The air was crisp with the sweet scent of apples and the pungent smell of manure. Everything added up to a perfect fall day in the small rural town of Dayton, Iowa where I grew up. It was a day that any boy my age would take their bike or a horse and travel to the local swimming hole where all the teenagers gathered to cool off and socialize.

There wasn't much to the town, one street, not even paved just dust and dirt was where the local farmer's market sat and placed fresh vegetables and fruit on stands outside for hungry children to pick up and regular customers to get their groceries. The local dentist, Mr. Schneider was also the town's barber and doctor. His shop was settled right next to the gas station where day after day Mr. Fritz would sit in his office waiting for travelers to stop by and ask for gas or even directions to get to Des Moines.

A few miles down the road was my father's farm. The farm has been in his family since the Civil War, but it was more of my farm than his as he passed away when I was fifteen from a heart attack in his sleep. I lived with my mother, Elizabeth and my younger brother, Dale, who was only five when my father passed. I had to run a farm by myself basically. When Dale turned eight, he couldn't do any of the hard labor yet, but he could groom the horses. He named all of them and that became his favorite chore, relieving some pressure and stress, off my daily schedule.

It was a beautiful fall day, but that one changed my life forever. The day was November 8th, 1942, and I was sitting in the living room listening to the evening news.

"In today's news around the world, German forces are still holding strong in Northern Africa. American and British forces land in the friendly country of Morocco where the German forces were unable to claim. And the German air campaign over Britain has stopped after almost two years of constant air raids and fire bombings. This news report is brought to you by the United States Army Recruitment Center. Uncle Sam needs you!" The radio reported what was happening in Europe and at the end, the lovely tune of Bing Crosby's "White Christmas" comes over the speaker and fills the room.

I hear the clinking of glass and porcelain coming from the kitchen where my mother and Dale are cleaning dishes and setting up for dinner. It felt like a regular Sunday evening with all the chores done before sundown, the soft, cool breeze entering the window behind the sofa where I was sitting reading the evening newspaper with the front-page saying how the German U-boats are sinking cargo and passenger ships in the Northern Atlantic.

"Dinner is ready!" My mother said peeking her head out of the kitchen with a red and white apron on covering her plain and dull blue dress that has seen its years of wear.

I picked myself up from the couch and gently fold the newspaper, placing it down on the table in front of me. Walking over to the dinner table, pictures of the family filled the wall adjacent to the steps leading to the two bedrooms. The pictures on the wall were of Dale, my mother, my father, and me. Some were of my mother's and father's wedding. The last picture of them together. My father tall and built, just like a typical farmer, and my mother in a long white gown. Back then she had long blonde hair that went a little past her shoulders, now it has turned to a dark brown. Her face was not as hard compared to now. Others were baby pictures of Dale, and the newest one was my graduation from Dayton High School where I graduated in the top twenty of my fifty student class. I walked over to my seat at the table and sat down, Dale already sitting, his gaze locked onto the meatloaf. My mother coming in from the kitchen with the last portion of our dinner, which consisted of meatloaf, corn on the cob, mashed potatoes, and fresh applesauce that my mother made from scratch.

"Let us pray." My mother said sitting down, straightening out her dress as her hands came together. "Lord, thank you for this dinner and for the strength that you have given this family. Please protect the young boys overseas who are fighting in the name of our Lord Jesus Christ, amen."

"Amen." Both Dale and I said simultaneously as his arms reached for the meatloaf and mine went for the potatoes.

"I heard Mrs. Simpson's son signed up for the Army yesterday," I told my mom as she placed a corn cob on her plate. Her face sunk, and her eyes lowered as she took a deep breath, releasing a heavy sigh.

"That is great, but you are not allowed to sign up. This farm needs you, I need you, and Dale needs you. I know boys your age want to go off and fight the Germans and the Japs, but you have more responsibilities here." Looking me directly in the eyes while placing a hand on Dale's shoulder interrupting his chewing of some meatloaf.

"But, Jonathan joined with the permission from his mother, and they have a larger farm than us."

"They also have worker hands who they pay!" My mother said slamming her hand on the table rattling the plates, her eyes filling with tears and cheeks blushing. "I will not let God take another piece of my heart away! I will not!"

Dinner went on, the only sounds were of forks hitting plates and throats allowing water to replenish us. Looking over at Dale, his eyes locked onto mine. The way his eyes looked were mixed with understanding and sadness. *Is Dale upset that I want to sign up or is he sad that Mom mentioned Dad?* Focusing back on my dinner I continued to eat what was left on my plate and did not dare to speak to my mother.

When everyone was done eating and left the dinner table to do their own things, I was tasked with cleaning the table and washing the dishes. My mother was in the living room listening to her favorite talk show on the radio and mending a hole in one of Dale's winter coats. He played with his toy trucks on the floor nearby, ramming them head-on, chipping paint and creating a metallic clink that ran through the house. My head was not full of anger while I wiped away excess mash potatoes off a plate, but of guilt.

Mother was right, I had to stay here and help. I could not let her and Dale struggle with the harvests and tend to the animals alone. Plus, I couldn't allow her to go through the sadness of losing me if I were to die. I wanted to slam the plate down into the sink. Releasing all the frustration that was built up inside seemed the necessary thing to do, but I knew that it would be wrong and only make the situation worse.

As I was finishing up with the dishes, I heard footsteps enter the kitchen. It was my mother who started putting things away. She was quiet at first, but her face showed that she wanted to say something to me, just not knowing how to say it exactly.

Placing a dinner plate into a cabinet, my mom turned to me, her face calm and settled, but her eyes showed concern and worry, "I'm sorry I yelled at dinner. I just can't bear to lose another loved one so soon. Your father died too young, and I don't want to end up like Mrs. Wether who lost her son last year. If you do feel that it is your duty to sign up and go fight for this country, then I can't stop you. For one thing, it will get you out of this tiny town, so you can actually see the rest of the world." My mother spoke in a tone that struck my heart and made me feel that she was willing to let her son leave and do something bigger than tending to a field all day.

"Tomorrow I'll go then and sign up at the recruitment office." The words came out tougher than I thought they would be.

I'll make you proud mom. Trust me.

"You can borrow the car to reach Flintown in time, but make sure the chickens are tended to before you leave. The fields will be fine, and Dale will look after the horses," she said, placing the last dish in the cabinet and turning to me smiling while still showing slight concern.

"Thank you, Mom. You won't be let down" I said, opening my arms and giving her a hug. Tears started to roll down my cheeks and soaked into my mother's dress. She must have noticed but didn't care and stayed focus on the emotional scene between us.

The day came when I was to enlist in the U.S. Army and fight for the freedom of all humanity. I reached Flintown, a town much bigger than Dayton, where most of the big-name stores are placed for the area. I pulled into a parking spot in front of the building where posters of Uncle Sam urging us to join and fight for the country filled the windows. His eyes and index finger seemed to point directly at me, filling me with confidence as I entered the recruitment center. Inside, the space was dull; posters and paintings covered almost all the whitewashed walls. Ten feet away was a large man, sitting at the front desk, writing something down. His shirt pressed flat, his tie perfectly straight, and medals shining on his chest were quite an intimidating sight.

You can do this; just tell the guy you want to volunteer. Taking a deep breath, I proceeded forward to the desk. My feet felt heavy, and my heart was pounding out of my chest.

The man looked up and placed down his pen, "May I help you, son?" His voice was loud and startled me though I never broke eye contact with him.

"I wanted to volunteer for the Army...sir," I told him in a shaky voice.

"Well, you came to the right place. Just complete this form right here, and then we will take your height and weight," The recruiter said, standing up to hand me a clipboard and a pen.

"Thank you, sir," I said reaching for the clipboard and then walking to a chair in the corner.

The form was simple, just asking for name, address, age, and what type of education I had. When the form was complete, I placed it on his desk as he looked up, nodding as a thank you. Then he stood up and walked over to a door.

"This way young man, time for your physical." The recruitment officer said gesturing me to follow him. "Please stand on the scale and I will get your weight."

I knew my body was fine, being a farm boy helps build muscles and hold the correct amount of weight. Everything went fine, my height and weight checked out. My health was perfect, and my spine was straight as an arrow. He then handed me a paper which was my acceptance form and told me to bring this next week when I go on the bus to basic training.

The week went by faster than I would have liked. As I was finishing buttoning my shirt, I noticed my door open from the reflection of the mirror. My mother quietly walked in, hands together and eyes glossy.

"Are you ready?" The words sounded painful coming from her. I nodded in response and followed her down to the car. Dale was waiting by the front door for us. His eyes glossy as well and hands folded with fingers running over each other.

My mother drove me to the bus stop where three other boys around my age were also waiting under the bus stop roof. I hugged Dale, ran my hand through his hair and kissed his forehead. I turned and looked at my mother who was on the verge of tears.

I hugged her and whispered in her ear, "I will come home safe, I promise you on that." Releasing from the hug, my eyes staring into hers. The pain and fear that rested inside of each eye almost put me on the verge of tears. I then kissed her on the forehead as I exited the car, grabbing my bag and started walking towards the bus stop.

I was no more than ten feet away from the car when I heard the slam of the car door close. I turned and saw my mother running towards me, "Joseph, wait!"

Turning around I was embraced by my mother, tightly hugging me, trying one last time to keep me home.

Her arms released me as my mother's eyes tried to persuade me to stay. I could see that she was imagining the little boy who would run around in the fields and hitch rides on the tractor with dad.

"Please be safe my child. I love you with all my heart and soul." The final words she would give me before heading off to training.

"I promise mother, I will be safe." I finished my promise and then gave her one last hug.

I turned around and continued walking to the bus stop, my mother doing the same back to the car. Each footstep was one closer to a new life, but also one further away from comfort and safety.

I could hear the car turn around and drive back down the dirt road. I pushed back the tears and tried to force out the images of my mother driving, tears flooding her eyes and creating rivers down her face, while Dale looks in the back window never losing sight of me.

I started walking over to the bus stop and waited with the other three guys who have been waiting for the bus to take us all from our hometown, all we really knew, to a more strict and serious lifestyle. Then off to war, where I may never see these three guys again or will come back with them and have a different life than what we left behind.

When I reached, the bus stop one of the men introduced himself to me, "Name's Winston, Winston Jones." The man said stretching out his hand. He was of average height and a little skinnier than I was. His blonde hair was cut short, and his blue eyes could have disappeared if they were put in the sky.

"Joseph, Joseph Warren. You from Dayton?" I asked trying to distract myself from the already shot nerves that made my stomach feel like millions of tiny knots.

As we finished shaking hands and before he could tell me where he was from, the sound of a Greyhound Bus rumbling down the street towards us interrupted the conversation. I felt a little at ease now knowing someone who I might stay by when we deploy. The bus pulled up, and the doors creaked open where a large man was sitting chewing what seemed to be tobacco.

"I don't have all day fella's, need to make one more pick up before heading to Camp Gabriel." The bus driver said waving us in.

As we took our seats, Winston sat next to me, and we chatted through the rest of the bus ride.

"So where are you from? We never got to finish that conversation." Looking out the window to the open fields and farm hands working with blue skies and the sun shining on their backs.

"I'm from McGregor, Iowa it's on the border of Iowa and Wisconsin. I come from a line of military officers, so I decided to continue that line." Winston continued to tell me about his father during World War One and his grandfather during the Civil War with their acts of bravery. "My father took out five German troops single handily when they charged into his trench. His superior honored him with a medal." His eyes lit up, dreaming of the day he would be honored a medal just like his father.

On the bus, there were a few guys my age and size, but others who were a little older and a lot more built, most likely working in steel plants or factories. The bus smelled of cow manure, but there was no option other than waiting it out. The bus took a sharp left turn down a small dirt road towards a forest, the road was rough and caused some riders luggage to bust open.

"Welcome to Camp Gabriel boys, home of the 528th Battalion, 2nd Regiment." The bus driver said smiling and stopping the bus in front of the woods, where an officer came out of the tree line.

The bus doors opened, and a short, but well-toned officer came aboard. "Welcome to Camp Gabriel, this is where I will train you and break you into a U.S. Army soldier. You will call me sir and sir only. Understood!" His voice booming inside the bus and rattling in my mind. From my view, I could see the spit flying from his mouth and peppering any nearby area. His eyes were a dark gray, his hair was a brown with blonde streaks racing around his head randomly, and his nose was more crooked than someone who worked on Wall Street.

"Yes, sir!" The voices of mine and twenty other men yelled back in sync.

"Now move, go...go...go!" The officer ordered us while shoving some of the men sitting in front of the bus.

My heart was already pounding, but I felt alive, more than I ever did before. Something inside of me turned on or off, and all the stress and anxiety drained out of my body. I was trying to hold back the smile that started to form on my face. When all of us got off the bus, we fell in line, it was a sloppy line, but that would change quickly. We then marched to our new home, which seemed to be in a forest, but the tree line was a decoy, once passing the tree line it turned right into an open field where tents and buildings littered the open range. General-purpose vehicles roaming around like flies in a dumpster and groups of soldiers marching and running into formation also packed the scene.

"Your group will be nicknamed Gold Company, remember that it may save your life one day. Now fall in and march to your bunks." The officer said looking directly at me, now fearing if my smile showed through. That day was the start of my life, my new life, the life that will forever change my body and mind.

When we reached the bunks, I was not caught by surprise like some other of the guys. The bunks were small, only a single cot was meant for each soldier with a footlocker at the end of it to hold all personal items. The inside of the building and even the beds smelled of mothballs and thick dust. *Well, looks like this is home for now.* Placing my bag on the cot and giving out a sigh of readiness.

Chapter II

Leaving Home

Weeks have passed since the day I entered basic training. Every week I wrote to my mother to inform her of my health and how rigorous the training was. That every morning Gold Company was ordered to run five miles in full gear, then we had to do drills of obstacles and go under barbed wire with live gunfire going on right above us. How Winston and I became best friends during training and how he wasn't from Dayton, but from a nearby town named, McGregor. We found that he and I had a lot of similarities; Winston also had a younger brother and lived on a farm, but his father was still alive and allowed Winston to join to follow the family's tradition.

We helped each other out during drills and the runs. We helped motivate each other as well as push each other to reach new gains.

When Gold Company finished basic training, we graduated with two hundred men. Our Captain whose name was Don George, but we never spoke his name, we all just called him Captain. He gathered us together and told everyone that we were given three days leave after basic training but had to report back here to not be charged with desertion.

The first morning of our leave was chaotic. Everyone had the same idea of getting breakfast then catching a bus to their town. After buying my ticket, I jumped on a Greyhound bus and went straight back home to see my mother and Dale to tell them about how training went and what I learned. The bus ride felt as though it was a twelve-hour ride instead of a two hour one. My excitement to come home overpowered any other emotions that came through my mind, like fear of what was to come next or how long the war would last.

When I got home my mother was helping Dale with the horses, a smile came across my face, seeing a simple life once again.

"Mother!" Yelling as I got closer to the barn. The brush she was holding dropped to the ground. Running to her as she did the same, we met in the middle and feeling the warm embrace of her almost broke me down to tears.

"I'm so happy you're home." She said never letting go of the hug until the right time came. Looking at me, her face went from joy to surprise, "They really know how to give a boy muscles." I never took notice, but when she said that I could see that my body did change, and my muscles increased a little more.

Before I could say anything back, Dale ran right into me wrapping his hands tight around my body, "I'm also happy that you are home, but why are you home?"

"Dale, don't be rude to your brother!" My mom hissing at his remark.

"It's fine mom, our Captain allowed us three days leave to visit our family and relax before they send us off." Once the words left my mouth, the expression on my mother changed for the third time. This time it was sadness and nervousness.

"Well, dinner is almost done, Dale go set the plates, your brother and I will continue to groom the horses."

Dinner felt like nothing changed, my mother made a stew with fresh bread bought from the farmer's market.

After taking a sip of water my mom turned to me, I knew something was wrong, but couldn't figure out what it could have been.

"What's the matter, mom?" I asked her, placing the glass down waiting for her news to come.

Her voice became soft, and her eyes started to become a glassy haze, "Mrs. Simpson's son...he was killed in North Africa by a German sniper. There's going to be a church service in his name later this week." I felt a large lump form in my throat, and a pit grow in my stomach.

"I wish that I could stay and attend the service, he was a good friend." Finishing up my dinner and excusing myself from the table. I headed to my room and laid on the bed thinking of his death, the war, and how I would do anything to keep my promise about living through the war.

The war came this close to my family, and I don't want it to get any closer. I grew up with Jonathan Simpson my whole life, we were neighbors and good friends. I can't believe he's dead now I tried to clear my head and proceeded to fall asleep.

On the third day of leave, I was helping my mother finish up the fall harvest. The ground was starting to get tough as mid-October was starting to show its signs. The sky started to become covered in a dull gray blanket of clouds, and the wind became mildly cold.

"Did your Captain say whether your company was to be sent to Africa or somewhere else yet?" My mother said looking at me in concern after placing some weeds into a handmade sack.

"No, not yet. But there has been talking around the camp about being stationed in England for some reason." I responded ripping some weeds myself out of the ground.

"Why England? Is the U.S. government worried about a German invasion of England?" My mother's eyes showed she was puzzled and slightly concerned while asking me those questions.

"I don't know yet, but I do think that my company won't see Africa at all," I told her trying to comfort her in a way.

That evening after dinner, I packed my things and said goodbye to my mother, this time for an unknown period. She didn't hold back the tears, neither did Dale, and myself.

"I promise to write to you often and pray every chance I get for my protection and the family's safety." Brushing back a lonely strand of hair, then pressing my lips to her forehead. "I love you, mom. Dale, make sure you help around. You are now the man of the farm, which makes this farm yours."

"I will miss you, Joseph. Be careful." Dale was trying to hold back tears and the urge to plea for me to stay home. I turned around and opened the door. The final time I would see them before experiencing war. I walked out the door and closed it behind me. Taking a deep breath, capturing the smells of the home before leaving. A rush of panic and fear ran through my body as the crying and heartache of my mother came through the door, but I kept walking knowing that leaving was the best option I had.

Months went by since my visit back home, and spring started to blossom all around. Training was harsh, and Captain kept the whole company learning how to jump out of a plane even in the dead of winter. Rumors were going around that Gold Company would become an airborne unit, and that sent my nerves on edge. I was born, raised, and grew up in central Iowa where the furthest I ever went was to Des Moines for a rodeo, but I never was in an airplane nevertheless jump out of one.

I was sitting on my cot when Winston walked over and stood in front of my bed, "Stand up soldier! Don't you know how to act in front of your officers?"

Jumping out of bed and standing at attention, confusion raced through my mind, but then I was surprised to see it was Winston and a smile broke through on the both of us, "Winston you got promoted to Sergeant?" The question was more of excitement and joy.

"Captain brought me into his quarters and promoted me. He said the reason for my promotion was by how strong of a leader I am." Winston told me while sitting on his cot next to mine. We celebrated the night by playing cards and talking about girls back at home.

A few days later I was sitting on my cot polishing my boots and finishing up a letter to my mother about how Gold Company was given the title of an airborne unit and how Winston became a Sergeant. I heard feet approaching the door and in came Winston with a surprised and excited look on his face while his walk also proved that he was full of joy.

"We are going to England! We deploy tomorrow and will be stationed over there for a few months training. Maybe we will meet some English gals!" He was telling me while pretended to dance around the barrack with an imaginary English girl. His feet gliding over the cold concrete floor, conducting random spins and hops.

"Do you know why we are going to England and not Africa with the rest of the American forces?" I asked turning down his excitement and stopping the dancing he was enjoying too much.

"Captain told me that we are part of a bigger plan that will turn this whole war around. Hitler won't see it coming." He said sitting next to me on my cot, looking me directly in the eyes making the information seem extremely important.

"Do you know when this might happen?" I asked a little concerned. My hands became sweaty, and my breathing started to grow shallow.

"In a few months. We will be training with some British forces as well. Whatever is going to happen, it's going to be big!" Winston said allowing the excitement to come back into his eyes and the dancing returned to his feet.

I could not sleep that night thinking of going over to England and training for something unimaginable. *Why did the army need airborne units so badly and why were they sending so many men to England instead of Africa where the fighting was happening?* After a few hours of thinking and looking up at the dim lit color of the barrack's ceiling I felt the warmth of sleep fall over me.

"*Warren wake up! We've been hit, German U-Boat struck our ship, and we are sinking!*" I heard the voice say as I woke up in a cold sweat, still on my cot. My breathing was heavy and my hands shaking. Winston and the others were sound asleep, dreaming of English girls, home, or their sweetheart welcoming them back after being gone to fight in the war.

"*Everything will be okay. The Navy will keep the U-Boats at bay, and we will reach England safely.*" I told myself, slowing my breathing down. I laid back down on my cot and closed my eyes letting the calming feeling of sleep take over.

My body was awoken by the sound of a bugle. My eyes cracked open to the morning sun peeking through the wide-open door giving everything a holy glow. Sitting up on my cot. My eyes caught the sight of Winston packing up his things for the journey to England.

"Rise and shine buddy, pack your gear and get ready to gather at oh eight hundred in front of the flag pole. We should be reaching England by the end of next week." Winston told me as my hands wiped across my face to help wake up somehow. I got up and started getting dressed while collecting my gear and personal items.

"I'll be ready by then...sir." Jokingly salute him and standing at attention with a big smile on my face.

We both laughed a little and helped each other pack up before meeting the rest of the company at the flagpole. When eight o'clock reached, all of Gold Company was standing in formation waiting for Captain to speak about why we are going to England.

Compared to my first day at basic training, we changed so much. Our formation was clean and sharp, every man was standing at perfect attention. In my mind, we were the definition of a true army company. While waiting for Captain to make his speech allowed the sun to conduct a beating down on my uniform, releasing sweat to trickle-down my forehead reaching my chin. For being mid-April, it was already hot out.

"Attention!" Winston's voice screamed notifying the company that Captain was approaching. We all watched as he walked in front of the flagpole, onto a makeshift stage so he can inform us. Captain was of average height, his uniform seemed too tight for his body, and his thick black hair combed back neatly gave the impression of oil slicks. His personality was nothing to reckon with as some men in the company called him "Bulldog" for his short temper, but I never got a chance to experience it. He was not that organized but knew exactly where everything was.

"At ease. Boys, you are all probably wondering, why we are being moved to England instead of Africa where the fighting is happening? And I will answer that question right now. The high command of both the British and the Americans have created an invasion plan of mainland Europe where Hitler and his kraut friends won't see it coming. England will be the launching point for this attack, and not just British and American forces will be training, but those of French, Belgian, and other free military armies that escaped the grip of the Nazis. As for Gold Company, we are tasked with being an airborne unit. Our true purpose has not been given yet, but I feel that we will be dropped into Europe to distract the Germans from the main invasion. This plan has been constructed and thought through for almost a year now. We will be making history boys, and I will be proud to fight by your side. Now go to the trucks and load up, we will be moving out once everyone is on. Dismissed." Captain finished his speech which left everyone with excitement and full of worry. I looked over to Winston where he smiled at me in excitement for what was to come. I was ready as well but also knew that the faces today would not be the same faces months or a year from now.

The roaring sound of fifty supply trucks waiting for all of Gold Company to get on board rattled my eardrums. My stomach was on edge, a concoction of excitement and fear. When sitting in the truck, my hands gripped my rifle to make sure it wouldn't fall out during the drive to the coast. My fingers kept pulling on the leather strap on my helmet to make sure it wasn't too tight. Everything seemed surreal from the movement of all two hundred men running around the camp, to the actual realization of going off to war now. All I knew and all I was will be staying here in Iowa, in America. The soldier I'm supposed to be and the man my mom will see me as when the war ends will be the result of what is to come.

It was a full day's trip to New York, but once we reached the city, it was chaotic. Not just our company, but other companies, regiments, and battalions were all filling into different ships being sent to England. Hundreds upon thousands of U.S. soldiers flooded the streets and alleyways of where the ships were being loaded.

I made a comment to Winston, "New York is tremendous. These buildings are taller than any building I've ever seen." Stunned by the sights and atmosphere of the city. Filling into one of the ships, we all waited for our departure to England. I was never on a ship, or on open water. *This may not go so well.*

The convoy of ships was massive, then again, I could have been looking at ten ships and thought the size would have been monstrous. There were at least seventy troop transport ships all fully loaded with five hundred men each. All the ships gathered after our departure from New York, some were from Boston, while others were from Virginia.

Escorting them were fifty destroyers, seven battleships, and twenty minesweepers. All of them were heading to England to start the first phase of what I thought was the biggest battle plan in all human history. The sea was calm for the most part, no storms or rough waves. The smell of salt water was more of a discomfort than pleasant. I, unfortunately, spent most of my time on the *U.S.S. Navigator*'s port hurling my inners out.

"Hey Warren, hanging in there?" Winston came behind me slapping me on the back forcing my stomach to release what was left of my lunch overboard.

"Yeah just peachy. You know how much longer-" I tried to finish my question, but the seasickness overpowered me.

"A few more hours. Just stay tight and don't be the first casualty of this company. I wouldn't want to fill out a form saying you died of sea sickness." Winston jokingly told me, pushing my head forward as he left me alone with the Atlantic Ocean.

The hours passed and England could finally be seen from the deck of the ship. Cheers rang out all over the convey. Fog horns blared as a way of celebrating too, I for one just wanted off that ship and onto land where I could keep some food down. When we got close enough to shore I gathered all my belongings and headed towards the side of the ship where the landing craft was acting as a colony of ants, helping one another with the main task at hand. Men were climbing over the side carefully placing each foot on the netting to not fall into the sea.

"Warren you're next, grab the side and swing over. One foot at a time and make sure not to fall overboard, I don't want to fish your ass out of the water." Captain said pointing to where I had to go.

"Yes, sir," I replied doing exactly what he said without the falling part.

The troop transport was a lot calmer than the landing craft which bounced over the smallest ripple in the water. There was nothing left in me to uptake, so that was the only positive. The landing craft was small; it could only fit twenty or so people without being packed. The sides were high enough to protect everyone's head from the splashes of crashing waves, and the driver had his own little protection from the waves as well with a small metal covering, acting as a roof over his position. The true meaning of the high sides and driver protection wasn't for the waves, but of incoming artillery shells and machine gun rounds.

The landing craft started to move forward and leave the side of the transport ship. Water was splashing and pouring into the craft, drenching everyone inside and proving that the tall sides of the craft were useless.

"Try and pour some of that water out of it will ya?" The driver yelled over the roaring of the engine and the crashing of the waves. We all took off our helmets and started scooping water out of the craft back into the ocean.

Once on land, everyone was scrambling to reform with their original companies. Luckily for me, I found Winston picking up a kid who fell from dehydration and wasn't as lucky compared to me who just couldn't hold down a single piece of food. A medic came over to aid the boy while Winston motioned for me to follow him.

Running over to Winston I said, "Hopefully we don't have to deal with water anymore."

"You're right about that, we will be flying for the next phase of this plan." He told me pointing at the sky. It was a calm blue, and the clouds were soft with some whisking along in the early summer breeze. There were also objects in the sky other than clouds, tiny black dots filled a portion of it. They reminded me of when Dale's pig was killed by a fox where the flies and maggots surrounded the corpse.

"Hey what is that?" I said patting Winston on the shoulder and then directing his gaze to the sky.

"That my friend is what will bring Hitler to his knees." He answered me with the biggest smile on his face. "Bombers from New Jersey. They flew all this way to be a part of this endeavor. Their purpose is to bomb anything deemed to be strategically valuable to the Germans. Tonight, after the officer meeting I'll tell you what will happen for the next phase, but for now, keep training and get your parachute landing down or you might break both ankles during the real thing."

"Understood," I told him

"Oh, from now on finish your sentences with sir when we are in public. I don't want Captain jumping down our throats if he sees us talking informally." He ordered looking me in the eyes.

"Yes, sir," I said giving his request the full respect it needed.

My eyes looked up one last time to the massive swarm of bombers overhead feeling a pleasant rush of comfort from the sight engulf my heart. I then proceeded to fall into formation with the rest of Gold Company who was formed up on the outskirts of the beach.

We then marched out towards our new living space which was Camp George. Marching through a tiny seaside village and through two miles of farmland, I felt more at home than I imagined. The rolling hills and the stone walls felt more out of a nineteenth-century painting than real life.

Maybe after the war, I can start a new life here. I thought to myself envisioning a small house looking out over acres and acres of farmland, while I watch my children play around, and help my wife hang out the laundry. With the memories of this war distant in my head.

Chapter III

The Calm Before the Storm

It's been over a year since I left home for the army. The date was June 1st, 1944 and England seemed to be more of a war machine than a country trying to defend itself from Hitler's claws. Camp Gabriel was buzzing with troops of not just American and British, but now Canadian and French nationalists joined the mix. Bombers and airborne planes littered the nearby fields, general-purpose vehicles were stationed everywhere, and on occasion, the horrific sounds of bagpipes could be heard echoing through the camp. One day, some of Gold Company including me and other parts of the American force taught the Brits how to play baseball and surprisingly they were fairly good, forgetting that cricket was close enough to baseball.

That night Winston went to the officers meeting to discuss the next phase of the plan. It was late at night, and my eyes were fighting my mind to stay awake. I did anything to stay conscious and settled on looking over my rifle. My hands were like a conductor of an orchestra, flawlessly and with precision cleaning my rifle just trying to keep my eyes open, waiting for Winston to come back with the information given during the officer's meeting. I could hear footsteps approaching as I locked the trigger guard back onto my rifle and racked the lever for where the clip went.

"Good and bad news buddy," Winston said busting through the tent's flaps walking towards his cot. "Which would you like first?" As he flopped onto his cot, releasing a loud sigh, signaling the tiredness overtaking him.

"Bad news," I told him feeling as though the good news was just as down weighted.

"Bad news is we will be jumping into Northern France behind enemy lines where we *think* the German's are least active and that we will be alone for a few days without reinforcements or support of any kind. Ready for the good news?" He said to me with enthusiasm hinting in the back of his throat.

"Well, I don't think anything can be worse than being surrounded by Germans for a few days so what is it?" I asked him with some concern, but enough confidence that it couldn't be that bad.

"The last phase is this week! We are jumping into France on the sixth." Winston's voice shot with excitement as he jumped towards me and grabbed both my shoulders, shaking me with a smile stretched across his face. That caused all drowsiness to escape my body and most likely his as well.

"Finally, we can get to see some action. I was getting tired of all the training, jumping, and hopefully different weather other than this damn rain." I told him looking outside where puddles of muddy rainwater formed around every structure and the visibility were only five feet.

"Tomorrow, Captain is going to give a speech to us, detailing what is happening and what our goals are," Winston informed me laying down on his cot tossing a baseball up above him with a blank stare into the abyss.

Wanting to go to sleep now I placed my rifle next to my bedside and turned over into my cot, "Goodnight Winston."

"Goodnight Warren." The sound of the baseball hitting the bottom of the tent and the creaking of his body adjusting in the cot were the last sounds my ears caught before my body was overcome by sleep.

The next morning all of Gold Company gathered in front of a general-purpose vehicle where Captain was standing on top waiting for the appropriate time to address his company. The sun was beaming down on us, the sky was a soft blue with swirls and mountain tall clouds painted on. The air held the smell of old rain from yesterday's shower, but a hint of sweet dew which lingered on the leaves and grass blades around the camp. Around me were now two hundred battle-ready soldiers who not only felt but showed they wanted action and to face the jaws of Hitler's army. To the left of me was a boy who looked extremely young for a soldier. His face soft and innocent, the bright blonde hair was combed back with a sleek gel look to it, and his helmet seemed two times too big, but he was a soldier like I was. Respect and loyalty flowed off his body making me feel as though he had a purpose, a reason other than to stop

Hitler, but I did not know what that driving factor was. As I pulled my gaze from the boy, Winston gave the order to stand at attention as Captain was about to start his speech.

"Today is the beginning of a new dawn. Where the events that follow will be stories, that will be told to your children and grandchildren. This crusade will not only be a reckoning for Hitler but salvation for all of the mankind. This company will be part of a massive invasion force targeted for northern France where the United States, Great Britain, and many other nations will land on the coast as well drop from the sky. As for our lovely company, we will be tasked to drop by parachute over a small village named Lisieux. High command informed me that the resistance there is not strong and should be an easy takeover. Even though we will have the element of surprise do not forget that one small mistake could be the deciding factor of living and getting a bullet. We will be jumping at night on June fifth and secure the village as well as nearby roads and bridges for the main assault that morning. I just want to say one last thing. All of you have been strong the past two years training and preparing for this. I am very honored to be the Captain of this company and would fight with all of you anywhere at any time. We will continue training tomorrow, but after that, it will be show time and a wakeup call for Hitler." His voice booming, bouncing off my chest and piercing my heart. Cheers and whistling roared after Captain finished his speech.

All of Gold Company was ready. I was ready for this endeavor into the unknown, where Germans will fight tooth and nail for each door, street, and every acre of France and any other country that we must push them back from. The thought tightened around my chest, my breathing quickened and became shallow. *"Calm down Joseph, you are freaking yourself out. Just breathe."* The images of Dale petting and grooming the horses, my mother placing seeds in the soft soil for next harvest flooded my mind, soothing my nerves and brought my breathing back to normal.

The next morning everything felt different, there was a thickness to the air, and everyone could feel it. The sun's rays were dancing through the camp and vanishing into the nearby forest, the sky was not a soft blue like yesterday, but a deep ocean blue where the clouds didn't seem painted on, but rather bouncing off the sky's color. My first thought was to write to my mother and tell her what's to come of me and this war. I walked calmly to the writing desk that

Winston and I shared, the paper neatly settled inside the typewriter prepared to be the messenger of anxiety and love for one's family.

June 4th, 1944

Dear mother,

By the time, you receive this letter I will already be in France fighting the Germans for control of some village. Gold Company is assigned to drop over a village on the night of the fifth. Captain says that resistance will be weak and that we will have the element of surprise on our side. We have been training for this over the past year and will be safe during my first engagement. I am still holding that promise that I made in the car before the bus came for Camp Gabriel. This war will come to an end soon, the way everyone is talking about the invasion and the number of soldiers and vehicles that are passing by daily prove that Hitler won't be prepared. Keep Dale away from the news reports for a while till the intensity drops, I don't want him having nightmares of his older brother being killed. Also, tell Dale I love him, that he is the best brother a man can ask for. And for you mom, start that book club you always talk about, get out of that house and enjoy yourself. Don't worry about me, I will be fine, and maybe dad will be watching over me.

Love always and forever,

Your son, Joseph.

The rest of the day was something special, from morning to afternoon Captain ordered us to train with running in the forest as well with practicing on our jumping and landing stance. My body was screaming for rest, my muscles were about to tear themselves apart, but all this training was meant for our survival, and I did not want to die.

When lunch rolled around my body could not be any happier. This lunch was a treat just like the sign out front of the cafeteria stated. Lunch consisted of pulled pork, corn on the cob, and two helpful slices of watermelon with a cup of sweet lemonade to wash it down. The cafeteria was just a large tent where tables and benches from nearby parks were set up just like any school cafeteria would be. The noise inside was as though a truck was driving by, everyone was excited about the next step starting tomorrow, others talking about home, while others like Winston were sad about leaving and missing all the English girls that he never got a chance to meet.

"I hope the Germans don't destroy every city and village, I would like to see some of France not torn by war," Winston told me while placing his tray down and sitting across from me where I was already scarfing down the lunch.

"You know they will be fighting tooth and nail for every inch of France. Just look at Italy and the defense they are putting up there." His face showed understanding as my reply entered his ears.

After lunch Winston, a few other American soldiers, and I wrangled a group of Brits to play one last game of baseball. Let's just say that we did not hold back and left the Brits in the dust with a score of fifteen to two. They fired back with a game of soccer, and that ruined our mood from our baseball victory. We all shook hands in fair sport and went back to our sides of the camp. Winston and I stayed in our tent the rest of the night and collected our thoughts for tonight.

The evening sun casting an almost halo effect over the camp giving us the sign that God was on our side. There was a slow warm breeze that brought comfort to the nerves of many including myself, and the songs the birds played added in on the soothing. It was almost as though God or just how the mind worked, but it seemed as if this would be the last time we would see beauty in nature or the peacefulness of an evening sunset. When the sun started to set, there was a magical moment that will be placed into my memory as one of the most amazing things I ever heard. A lonely bagpipe started playing a soft tune, echoing through the camp. Then the voices of British troops singing a song to match the tune. The song sounded familiar, but I couldn't put my finger on it. Some American soldiers also recognized the song better than me and started singing along as well.

"Winston, do you hear this? The whole camp is singing." Both him and I were quiet, enjoying the soft melody that was running throughout the camp, then more bagpipes joined in and more men started singing. Eventually, the whole camp started singing out loud to the tune till nightfall. My mind raced with a million thoughts on what is to come and how my life has played out so far. Looking over to Winston I knew he was thinking the exact same things.

As my eyes retracted from the opening in the tent and my ears dropping the lowering sounds of the song, I returned to my book, but not long did Winston's voice catch my attention instead, "Hey Warren, are you ready for tonight?" sitting upright in his cot polishing off his boots.

"A little nervous. I just don't know what to expect so that kind of helps. Also, I don't really like to imagine what will happen or what might. Usually, my mind goes to the worst possible scenarios." My reply straightforward trying to kill the conversation and get back to my book.

"Guess you will find out in six hours." The words hitting my stomach harder than a direct punch. Twists and knots started to form, my breathing quickened, and I could not concentrate on the book in front of me. Closing my eyes and picturing back home with Dale and mom. Helping her set up the table for dinner and pretending to throw Dale in with the pigs eased my nerves and calmed by breathing.

"Just wake me up when it's time," I told Winston, placing the book down on the stand next to me and turning on my side to get comfortable. Closing my eyes to keep my nerves in check as well to start the long process of trying to sleep knowing that there may be a possibility that in six hours I would be lying on a random French street with a bullet in the chest and a puddle of blood surrounding me.

"*Green light! Go...Go...Go! Warren watch-*" The explosion jolting me awake, but I was still in my cot. A cold sweat covering my body and my throat was painfully dry. Luckily for me, it was time to prepare for the next and final phase of this invasion.

As I sat up on my cot, Winston was already dressed and in full combat gear. Him standing there with a helmet covered in a mesh netting, the olive drab jacket with a brown sand backpack holding his parachute, and his rifle in pristine condition slung over his soldier barrel facing upwards made me come to full realization that it was time and this time it won't be for practice. This time I would be jumping out of a real plane, most likely under AA fire into enemy territory.

"Ready?" Winston asked me, a hint of concern or nervous coming through in the question. His face was calm and collected, but his eyes showed even in his *relaxed state* that we were both equally scared of what was to come next.

"I don't have any other choice, but yes I am ready." Telling him while taking a deep breath and putting my helmet on, now fully dressed in combat gear. "Let's give Hitler a surprise gift." Taking all my positive feelings into a smile and joke. It made

Winston smile and chuckle allowing the tense atmosphere to lower the pressure a few levels.

Exiting the tent was not just the fact that we were leaving the last safe place for a few months or even a year, but it was also the fact that once we board the plane, all our families and neighbors and countries will be looking towards us for protection against Nazi Germany and its ugly boot. That the war is not just in North Africa and Italy, but now it will be in the heart of Europe with too much riding on the success of a single invasion.

Chapter IV

D-Day

The cool midnight air held enough chill for the air being exhaled visible and the moon casting a bright glow as if it were acting as the sun. The walk seemed endless, but it also felt good for taking so long as it did.

"I always wanted to ask you this, but does this invasion have a name to it? It seems too big just to be a normal invasion." I asked him while walking through a field of knee-high grass to the airfield that stationed the planes.

"It's Operation name is Overlord. The sea invasion has its own operation name, and that is Neptune, like the Roman God of the sea. Warren, this invasion is the biggest in human history. No other war has seen this large mass of troops prepare for an invasion like this before." The words of this being the biggest invasion in history gave me a jolt of excitement knowing that I will be a part of history.

As we reached the airfield the moon's light dancing across the wings of over one hundred planes both propeller and glider. The metallic shine was almost blinding but still illuminated the ground well. The foot traffic of different airborne divisions filing into aircraft made the area feel small and cramped. As Winston and I grouped up with the rest of Gold Company on the front part of the airfield near three C-47s, we waited for the instructions given by Captain. The cool air was a relief for my nerves, and the orchestra of crickets allowed the unknowns of war to be washed away.

"We will be split up into seven teams, each team designated a different plane. Once we drop into France all hell will break loose, rendezvous point will be the village square. The German's don't know that we are dropping into their village until the fighting starts, so get to the ground safely and quickly find a partner. It will stay dark and recognizing friend from foe will be hard. The code word question will be Ruth,

and the response will be Yankees. Understood?" The
Captain giving everyone their last intel before the
invasion started, his face masked by the dark of night,
but his voice sounded confident enough for us to feel
ready.

"Yes, sir!"

"Alright, move 'em out."

All two hundred men started marching towards
war and possibly death. I got into line boarding one of
the planes that were on the left side of the leading
one. There were no steps to help get into the aircraft,
only two metal bars on either side of the opening to
allow a support. The inside reminded me of a soup
can. All metal frame with one long row of benches on
either side. The inside smelled of mothballs bringing
me back to when Dale and I had to put mothballs in
the guest room during the winter to protect the
sheets. A single red light hanging from the ceiling near
the exit like a bat in a cave, giving us the only source
of visibility inside the plane. I took a seat in the middle
of the aircraft as Winston sat across from me, smiling
and resting his rifle against his inner thigh.

When the guts of the plane were filled with the
max amount of eager battle-ready soldiers, the
engines roared to life, startling me as the noise was

greater than expected. The engines getting to speed forced the plane to move forward, jolting me to my right bumping into the kid that back at the beach near Camp George collapsed from dehydration. This time though I could see the softness in his face, the roundedness of his button nose, and the large size of his not grown in ears. His brown hair peeking through his plain olive-green helmet and his what I assumed were blue eyes looking directly forward into a pit of emptiness. Before long the C-47 was in the air and climbing higher into the sky where in three hours the realization of war will be met.

The flight was quiet, no loud talking or laughing. A prayer or two could be heard once and awhile as well with the chewing of gum or tobacco. The scent of mothballs was replaced with the terrible memory smell of salt water as we were over the channel. Winston held his rifle tight with his eyes closed and his breathing slow paced. A guy next to him was looking at a picture of his wife giving the picture one final kiss before being put in the pocket of his jacket next to his heart.

"One hour!" The co-pilot announced tilting his head into the hull of the plane rattling the calm of some men.

Freezing shocks ran through my body, chilling my blood and forming knots in my stomach.

Calm down, just do what Captain said and you will live. Just close your eyes and breathe slowly. The voice inside of my head trying to untie the knots and unleash the massive pressure buildup.

My eyes and lungs listened to the voice, images of explosions and gunfire filled my head, forcing to change the image my imagination created a vivid picture of the farm during a spring morning. The morning mist hugging the ground as the golden sun sparkled the dew blanketing the grass. Drowsiness flooded my body and unconsciousness was welcomed as well. I just hoped that waking up would occur before the jump and not after our plane would be shot by AA fire.

"Warren wake up. Ten minutes before our jump." A voice recognizable and a gentle shove on the shoulder woke me up from a well-needed nap. My eyes opened, Winston looking directly at me, cast in a blood red from the standby light. My hands running over my eyes trying to gather the surroundings better. Rifle still resting in between my legs and the strap on my helmet a tiny loose. A helpful tip from Winston who before at training told me that if your strap is too tight the initial force of your parachute opening would cause the strap to snap your neck. The boy next to me looking down now, taking deep breaths and the man next to Winston was also waking up from his nap.

"Stand up...hook on!" Captain said motioning us to stand up and hook on our clip for when we would jump.

In just two minutes from Captain's order to standby, all hell broke loose. Explosions rocked the plane left and right, flashes from outside illuminated the inside of the plane. The force of the flak explosions echoed through my body.

Turn green, please turn green. My mind screaming as my eyes never lost contact with the red standby light bathing us in a blood red.

"Green light! Go...Go...Go! Winston go, Lawrence go, Warren go!" Captain yelling while pushing us out of the plane. Reaching the door, the night sky was reduced by the immense light coming from AA fire, machine gun rounds trying to pick off soldiers, and the flames of a burning engine on the plane next to us falling out of the sky. Men still jumping out, not for the mission, but for their lives. The village below looked almost peaceful surrounded by the scenes of war. Spotlights intruded my vision as I took the leap out of the plane and into the fray.

The initial jolt out of the plane was horrible, but the slow fall down to Earth was even more terrifying with machine gun rounds and small arms invisible to the eye but sounded deadly. I could look up past the canopy of the parachute to the image of my plane flying as more men jumped out, then an explosion shattered the left-wing tilting and then spinning the plane to the ground. Fear ran through my body, looking down I could see the ground running up to meet me, other men already landing, some landing in trees, others were taken by the wind and landed somewhere in the village. One poor soul that hoping wasn't Winston landed twenty yards away from an AA emplacement. Before he could grab his rifle, the Germans had cut him down. The landing was hard, but I rolled and managed not to break my ankles in the process.

All the sounds of war somehow vanished, the night sky was filled with stars that I have never seen before, the bright full moon giving some light to the battlefield. Flashes of yellow and orange from AA guns with a handful of planes falling to the ground not able to withstand the amount of damage they took. My surroundings were familiar, just like in England there

were acres and acres of pasture, a small dirt road was
about a hundred yards away with a fence parallel to
either side. A single tree next to the road with a
soldier hanging from his snagged parachute most
likely dead as his body did not move. The village was
to my left in the distance silhouetted by the moon's
light and lit up by the firing of the German anti-aircraft
guns for seconds at a time and machine gun fire. The
village held houses hugging one another two stories
high with a church steeple towering over the rest of
the village. To my right, more soldiers landed and
grouped up together to have some protection and
strength for an attack on the defenses of the Germans.

Running over to them I noticed that they were
not Gold Company.

"What company are you with?" I asked one of
the men loading his rifle with a clip while two others
tended to a wounded comrade who seemed like he
broke or twisted his ankle on the landing.

"Easy Company, they're with Mike Company,
and the lad on the ground is with Baker. My name is
Lee, Sargent Lee." The man said pointing towards the
individuals as he announced which outfit they were
with. "Which one are you with, guessing everyone got
mixed up during the jump?"

"Gold Company, have you seen anyone from that around?" Looking at the man from Easy Company as constant explosions of anti-aircraft guns went off.

"Unfortunately, not. We will stay together and take out some AA batteries for the next wave of paratroopers. After that, push into the village and meet at the center. From there what companies are scattered will regroup at the church." Sargent Lee said as the two other men stood up and told the wounded one that he will be okay and that he is safe.

The four of us moved across the open terrain, making quick movements from one dead cow to the next for cover. The stench was appalling, but it was the only source of cover if we wanted to get close enough to those battery positions. The nearest AA gun was forty yards away and no cover between us and the gun. The air wasn't cool anymore. Instead, a warm, smoky wind came through. The screams of men who landed too close to the enemy and the sounds of small arms fire surrounded my position. Bullets whizzed by as a group of Germans spotted us and laid down tremendous fire, pinning us behind a corpse of a cow now being peppered with bullets.

Stay calm, breathe, just pull the trigger a few times and duck back down. Launching up from my prone position I lined up on a German and pulled the trigger. The screaming of the barrel as my first round left the gun and flew, entering the German. His body dropping quick and out of sight behind a pile of sandbags.

My first kill, the first of probably many human lives I could take during how many months. My gut went hollow, and my throat dried up like a puddle in a July heatwave. He most likely didn't see me pop up or the flash of my gun, all he knew was something entered his body, and it created tremendous pain before his organs failed him. After going back behind the cow, questions raced through my mind. *How old was he? Was he forced into the army or did he love Hitler that much? How will his mom find out about her son's death? Will they tell her that savage Americans fell from the sky and massacred everyone in the village or tell her that her son took on a group of Americans single-handedly and died a true hero?*

On me were two smoke grenades and three hand grenades. My rifle held ten rounds, now nine and five clips stashed in a pocket of my jacket. The gun emplacement that pinned us down was in range for a grenade, but throwing it demanded an accurate toss into the circle of sandbags.

"Give me cover fire!" I yelled over the now intensifying battle around the village to the three men next to me.

"Got it! Covering fire!" Sgt. Lee ordered to the other two men. All three poking over the corpse and released their full mags into the enemy's position giving me a few seconds to grab a grenade, pull the pin, and throw it into the circle of sandbags. Reaching for the grenade my fingers wrapped around the pin and yanked it out of its holding slot. I released the lever and tossed the grenade into the air hoping to land right on top of the AA gun. All four of us went back down behind the now shredded corpse of the cow to protect ourselves from the explosion. Two seconds went by before the grenade went off and the short screams of the enemy signaled the grenade landed perfectly taking out all five members of the battery. Six kills in a matter of ten minutes, I did not want to imagine what the number would be in five weeks.

Right after the explosion we bolted across the forty yards and threw ourselves against the pile of sandbags where my first kill was shooting from.

"How many AA guns are around here Sarg?" One of the men from Mike Company asked in between gasps of air, clutching his rifle for dear life.

"I don't know, but let's try and take one more out before pressing our advance into the village streets," Lee replied pointing towards another AA battery which ceased fire as the team got into cover and started shooting at us with their rifles and MP40s. "I'll take this one." Unpinning one of his grenades and flinging it into the air as it burst right behind the five Germans who all fell forward against the sandbags not moving afterward. "Okay, now move into the village and make our way to the church."

The crackle of machine gun fire echoed through the night as the night sky flashed of explosions and distant artillery rounds. The fighting leaked into the village as door by door fighting accord. We made our way into a small street that was made of dirt, and the houses were pinched together with gray limestone creating the front walls. All of us were on high alert passing by a dead soldier hanging from a house where his parachute got caught by the shingles of the roof. His body littered with bullets, head slumped looking towards his rifle lying broken on the ground. Traveling down the street in a single file line,

Lee in front, the two guys from Mike Company, and I were coming up the rear.

"Get down!" Lee screamed as a German machine gun fire chipped away the wall next to us and killing the guy behind Lee instantly. The other guy from Mike Company laid down covering fire while Lee and I ran to the other side of the street to take cover behind a staircase. "Lay down covering fire so he can get over here."

I nodded in return standing up and pulling my trigger erratically. The exchange of gunfire was so great no one could cross the street without getting hit. When my clip sprung up notifying me that I had to reload, Lee gestured towards the other guy who was lying prone behind his dead friend to come over here. My new clip was in and brought my rifle back to firing out rounds. Turning my head for a second, my eyes caught a glimpse of the soldier getting up and taking three steps before being cut in half by the German machine gun. His helmet rolling off his head towards me, his body sprawled out on the dirt road as a puddle of blood grew underneath.

"Damn it! You cowards!" Lee screamed poking up and emptying his clip then right after pulling a grenade and tossing it towards a metal grate flush with the ground where the machine gun was. The grenade rolled perfectly into the room, and a billow of smoke followed an explosion. Lee jumped from our position and charged the area where the enemy was. Standing right in front of the metal grate he let out a barrage of bullets into the room.

I stood up from behind the staircase and started walking slowly towards Lee who was now leaning against the wall crying. My mind also wanted to breakdown from what already happened in just a matter of an hour.

Putting a hand on Lee's shoulder, while looking into his eyes I said, "It's going to be alright. We just need to get to the church and meet up with everyone else. Just keep strong, and maybe we will run into another squad of random soldiers."

He nodded in reply wiping tears from his face with the back of his hand. His face was hard, a chiseled jawline already covered in dirt and dust from the battle. His eyes were a dark blue and lips thin. When he took off his helmet to get some sweat off his face, I could see that he had a dark red hair cut short and soaked in sweat.

"I never knew their names." Lee's words felt as though a bullet went right through my chest. How many other boys died today without being known by name?

"It will be alright. The church is two blocks away, I only have one clip left and two grenades, plus two smoke grenades. We should have enough ammo before reaching the church. Will you be okay?" Comforting him and asking to ensure he was stable enough to not get us both killed.

"Yeah, I'll be fine. What's your name?" Lee asked standing up placing his helmet on his head. The sounds of war still around us, yet the peacefulness of the little street we were in blocked out those horrors.

"Warren, Joseph Warren," I replied looking around to make sure we were still safe.

"Well, Warren, let's get a move on," Lee said walking towards the next block as I followed in suit our rifles pointed in the direction of our movements, ready to take down any foe that came our way.

The village must have been peaceful before Hitler, and his armies came in, ruining and destroying everything. The people of this village seemed to live a simple life from just looking around, small shops and bakeries, offices of many kinds scattered throughout the blocks we walked. The night sky was starting to fade by the warming embers of the morning sun. The darkness of night retreating into the cracks of the village while the sun's rays flooded the streets and alleyways.

When Lee and I were turning the corner, a familiar voice yelled out, "Ruth!"

"Yankees!" I screamed in reply, happy enough to know they were friendlies and not enemies. The familiar voice now revealed the dirt covered body of Winston who had a thin line of blood trickling down his forehead. A large smile stretched across my face and pressure released from my shoulders.

Winston was leading a squad of mix matched soldiers but had more Gold Company than any other. Lee recognized one of the men Winston was with and ran over to him and gave a hug.

"Easy Company got scattered across the village, but most of us managed to capture the village square. Baker Company is securing the left side of the city and Gold Company is sweeping the right. All AA batteries were taken out in the first hour of the fight, we captured about twenty Germans, but our casualties were heavy. Mike Company took the most in the initial jump with most of their planes going down." A guy from Easy informed Lee and I as we started walking towards the church with everyone else.

"How many did Gold lose?" I asked concerned knowing the plane I was in also went down.

"About thirty-five. Captain is still alive and is at the church now thinking of the best defensive positions for a counter-attack." Winston replied with a solemn look. "A lot of brave boys and men died tonight, some didn't even see action. The boy you were sitting next to on the plane was with me. We were walking down a street with six other guys, and a squad of Germans turned into our street. Both of our parties were caught by surprise, and he was the first to get hit, I laid down covering fire for the medic to grab him. But he was dead before the medic could drag him to cover. A bullet went right through his head above the left eye."

My eyes started to fill with tears, but I held them back to control my emotions. When we got to the village square, the scenery changed. The church was in ruins, the steeple was still towering over the village, but large chunks of the wall and stained glass littered the ground. Rubble piles and small fires crowded the open square. By the front of the church, Captain was leaning over a table with maps sprawled out and two other officers with him, most likely from the other companies.

The morning sun was now over the horizon and the night sky transformed from a soft pink to a bright blue. Light smoke clouds stretched over the village from where downed planes crashed and AA guns destroyed. Bodies of both sides scattered the village streets while some American bodies laid across the open fields or hanging from trees. For me, I was taking a seat inside the church praying for the wellness of my family and my protection through the war. Inside were others praying for their protection and grieving the loss of a friend.

"...amen." I finished my prayer just in time for Winston to sit behind me leaning forward and resting his crossed arms on the back of my bench.

"This is going to be a bloody war I can sense it already," Winston said eyes concentrated on the statue of Jesus being crucified red paint sliding down his legs resembling the blood lost from his sacrifice.

"This war has been bloody and will just keep getting even more. How long do you think before the Germans counter-attack?"

"Soon, probably later today or tomorrow. The sea invasion should be starting now or already commencing. Once the main invasion force pushes the Germans this far back, we will cut off their retreat and link up with the main forces."

I looked one last time at the statue of Jesus, creating a cross with my hand motion and stood up grabbing my rifle next to me and walked out of the church with Winston behind me. Our boots echoing from the polish stone flooring and the quietness of a now ruined church. When we got outside the summer's sun was heating up the air and making it almost uncomfortable to be in full gear. The sky a perfect blue with only small faint clouds, the smoke was now gone, and men were moving all around the village to create defensive positions and gather ammo and weapons from fallen comrades and enemies. I could see men walking, carrying stretchers down a road to one of the fields where we created a makeshift cemetery for the dead. The main office building was converted into a field hospital, and two houses down from it was the officer's quarters where all the captains and lieutenants stayed.

"What is the official casualty list?" I asked curiously more than worried.

"Ninety-seven in the fields and village, unknown for the ones that didn't get out of their planes before they crashed, but that is just our company. I don't know about the others yet. We were able to capture twenty Germans, and their casualties were around one hundred and twenty with fifteen wounded."

Over two hundred and seventeen men died over the course of one night. My stomach turned and flipped before I knew it I was bent over hurling my breakfast of biscuits and bad coffee onto the dirt road. War was cruel but never expected it to be this cruel.

"You okay Warren?" Winston asked concerned patting me on the back to reinsure me that even with death around us, there will always be someone to comfort us.

"Yeah, thanks though," wiping my mouth and catching my breath.

After throwing up Winston and I walked down to the east side of the village where Gold Company was stationed. There was one road leading in and out from the east with a bridge two hundred yards away. On either side of the road next to the outskirts of the village were two machine gun emplacements. Both fully armed and ready for any attack, they even managed to plant explosives on the bridge just in case if our position becomes overrun. The buildings next to the machine gun nests were stocked with soldiers who bunked and used them as an extra layer of defense. We had two rocket launcher teams stationed on either flank of our defense, and each company had a spotter held up in the bell tower for a better view of our surroundings. The village was quiet, no one was in a joking or talking mood after last night.

We walked passed two houses already full of men. The houses seemed to be made of limestone as the ones closer to the church were made of brick. Winston showed me to the house where I would be staying with other privates and low-ranking soldiers.

"It's nice inside, even though the German's lived here for a few years. It's not in bad shape, and all the beds are comfy," Winston told me with a smile while opening the door which leads to a large living space full of vintage furniture and simple oil lamps all resting on what used to be polished wooden floors. A dusty, full bookshelf hugged the wall on the left side while a staircase leaned on the right wall. Upstairs were three dull bedrooms each holding two beds and a dresser. The first two bedrooms were occupied by soldiers either sleeping, reading, or looking at their weapon. The one furthest in the back of the second floor was empty each bed perfectly made and untouched for possibly two years. A thin layer of dust lingered on the dresser and coated the floor, but I did not care. Back home there would always be a line of dust even after cleaning. A window with parted dark red curtains let in the afternoon's sun. The view was of the road leading towards the bridge. A small creek ran under the bridge and gave the scene a picturesque feeling. In the distance past the bridge held the beginning of a light forest. If it weren't for the fact that we were in the middle of a war and that behind me was the destruction of a village, I never would have known that there was a war going on by looking out that window.

I looked around my room again this time for tactical reasons. "*If any attack were to happen I could take a position in my room with more cover. Most likely take cover behind the windowsill and shoot out the window.*" Thinking of an imaginary swarm of Germans coming over the bridge while I take a position in my room targeting them one by one before they started to retreat.

I stayed in the room laying on the bed which was the most comfortable thing I've been on since I signed up for the Army. Thoughts ran through my mind, and so did questions. *"Did the naval invasion succeed, if so how far did they push inland? If it was a horrific loss than what will all these airborne divisions do? Will my mother ever know from the news reports that I'm still alive and not of the many that died in the first few days?"* With the sun glistening through the window, painting the back wall and bed with a golden yellow my eyes closed and allowed sleep to take over my body. The first time in over twenty-seven hours.

Chapter V

Recovery

When my eyes opened, and no light was shining through the window, I knew it must have been night or late evening. Rubbing my eyes with the tips of my fingers I got out of bed still fully clothed with helmet and rifle leaning next to the bed on a nightstand. Standing up my muscles were strained and tight. Knowing I would have to get over it, I reached for my rifle and helmet, then walked down the stairs to the front door. Reaching for the door knob, I was jolted back by the swift opening showing Winston wide-eyed.

"German forces coming in from the north. Either a counter-attack or the forces in retreat from the beach. Get defenses up and pre-" Winston was thrown into the house from the impact force of a mortar round and collapsed on top of me. The explosion landed down the street about twenty yards from the door creating a crater in the middle of the road and shredding the walls of houses facing the impact.

"Didn't hear that coming." Winston jokingly said to me as the other guys in the house started running down the stairs to join us. "Okay, the enemy is coming from the north, we don't know if this is the retreating forces or a counter-attack. Baker Company is holding them for now, but Gold was ordered to reinforce that position. We need to hold this village at all costs. No armored vehicles spotted, but we do have anti-tank teams stationed just in case. Now move! Warren follow me." Everyone started running out of the house, Winston and I ran towards the church while the other four were running down a different street to help Baker Company repel the German force. Mortar rounds were exploding all around sending debris flying everywhere. Houses were being ripped apart, and small arms fire blasted throughout the night.

"How large is the attacking force!" Yelling over the mortar explosions to Winston running down the street as the sounds of gunfire increased with every step forward.

"Fairly large, I guess it's the retreating forces from Normandy. Which for our luck means friendly forces are about two hours away if they keep pushing through the night. If not, they will be here by early morning."

We reached the church where Captain and twenty other men from Gold Company were rallied at the front of the church lit by the moon hanging high above a village that has seen too much bloodshed in such little time. The frontline of the battle was three blocks down from the church, and from here bullets could be heard whizzing by. Most of us had wood stock Springfield rifles, Winston and Captain held Thompson machine guns, and the bravest of us all was the man who carried a rocket launcher.

When we saw no other man from Gold come to the church Captain decided it was time to move. "Alright, boys, double time it to the most western edge of the village, we will hold that position and then start to advance with a sweeping motion to the east where the enemy will start to crumble and hopefully surrender." He said to us while indicating a sweeping motion with his hand just as a mortar round exploded on top the church's roof shaking the steeple, but it was still stood. A dust cloud rushed out from the front doors and surrounded us in a thick gray cloud of smoke and dust. "Let's move. Now!"

We all started running down a small road leading to the west side of the village, the crackling of rifles and the repeating sounds of machine guns overpowered the heavy breathing that was coming out of my mouth. Mortar rounds were exploding left and right sending debris into the road and leaving houses destroyed. My rifle stuck to my hand as my other hand was making sure to keep my helmet on my head. Behind me a mortar went off right next to a wall, I turned to see the explosion sending shrapnel and debris into the road catching three guys in the process and killing them instantly.

When we reached the most western edge of the village a group of fifteen Germans came out of the forest on the other side of the field.

"Get behind the stone wall!" Winston ordered as I ran to the wall, hitting my side on it from dropping too fast. I collected myself and raised my rifle over the wall. Looking down the sights, I locked on an enemy who was trying to get behind a hay mound. Squeezing off the trigger my rifle flashed, and my eyes closed. When my eyes opened, I saw the body of the man I shot lay face down on the ground dead. I kept up with the fight and fired off three more shots before Captain ordered us to cease-fire.

My mind was a blur, I could not think only react as we held our position for what seemed like forever. Then movement came from the forest and flashes lit up the field in front of us.

"Open fire!" Captain cried out as another group of Germans rushed towards us. The whole line opened fire, causing the wall to light up from the flashes of the rifles as the sound of church bells ringed around us was that of hollow bullet shells hitting the stone wall. Winston was next to me on my left reloading and then going back up to repel the never ending German attack, but on my right, was a man who got a direct hit on his shoulder.

I stopped shooting and rushed to his aid, "What do you need me to do?" My voice panicking not from trying to save the man's life, but also from the German force that wanted to destroy us.

"I don't know. Keep up the fight I'll be fine.' The man said pressing his bloodied hand on the wound to slow down the rushing of blood. I moved back to where I was shooting and continued to repel the attack.

The screams of the wounded were more painful than a bullet, and the worst part was that our squad didn't have a medic on hand, so they just had to keep the pressure on themselves. Some passed out from the pain and fear, while others died from blood loss and organ failure.

I regained my composer and lined up my next shot, but my body was thrown against the wall, dazing me. Everything went slow, and the sounds were distorted, looking to my left I saw Winston get up and tackle a German who jumped over the wall. Winston took out his knife and got on top of the soldier who was trying to stop the incoming blade. My eyes kept closing and reopening changing the sequence in hand to hand combat that started to form around me. When I regained focus, Winston plunged the knife into the German's chest as the enemy soldier pleaded for his life, while other comrades around me were also dealing with their own combat and life-saving situations.

When I tried to get up, a German soldier jumped over the wall, forcing the end of his rifle into my face. I fell back down, this time out of breath. The German took out a blade and prepared to kill me. Trying to fight back, I kept pushing and shoving his arms away from me. *Please God not like this, anything but this. Mom, I'm sorry that I couldn't hold the promise, keep Dale safe and comfort him. I love you.* Tears started to distort my vision, then the sound of gunfire and the feeling of the German who was on top of me shake. When my vision came back into focus, I could see Winston standing next to me with his gun pointing to where the German was. Now my almost killer was laying on the ground, face up eyes open and with multiple gunshots pumped into his chest.

"Hey, buddy you okay?" Winston asked picking me from the ground and handing me my rifle and helmet.

"Yeah, I'm fine. Why did the gunfire stop?" Asking in a way that Winston thought the sound of gunfire was heaven to my ears, but not meaning it to be said that way.

"Most of the attacking force died and after that hand to hand combat some ran off back into the woods," Winston told me as we started walking back to the church to regroup with everyone else. Some men stayed behind to tend to the wounded, but some would be of little use.

The village did not seem the same the night I jumped out of the plane, the peacefulness of it, the simplicity, and the quietness untouched by the surrounding actions of war. Now butchered and burnt by two nights of constant fighting with roads covered in blood and debris, houses disintegrated, and the beautiful church that laid in the center now destroyed from mortar rounds last night. There were too many bodies to count, and some still crowded the roads and fields.

My mind felt out of place that I could not think only react and this created fear that surged throughout my body. When the life of my first kill was taken away by my hands, I felt uneasy, but now walking the streets and seeing a soldier with no leg or his intestines spewing out did not phase me.

Is this what war causes, not just death and destruction, but the absence of caring for human life?

The village square was crowded with men from different companies, eager to have a few days' rest as the main force pushed forward. I wanted to keep fighting but knew rest was the best option. No one was clean faced, everyone either had dirt, blood, bruises, cuts, or bandages. Winston's face was covered in dirt and blood, but not his, rather that of the German he stabbed when we were on the wall. Everyone's eyes were the same hollow, emptiness to them. Hope and the preservation of life were taken away in just forty-eight hours, I had a feeling that my eyes looked the same.

A loud whistle engulfed the eerie silence, Captain looked up to the steeple where a soldier was giving out hand signals.

"Armor vehicles. Infantry, five divisions. Coming from the northwest. Americans." Captain said out loud so the rest of us could understand what the scout saw. The silence was changed by cheers and yells, Winston ran over to me with a smile I could only remember as the day he told me we were going into phase three of the invasion and hugged me.

"Do you know what this means?!" He asked me, releasing me of the hug and holding me by the shoulders, looking me in the eyes. The hollowness still lurked in them, but the cheerfulness of his sky-blue eyes showed more.

"We don't have to fight for a few days and rest?"

"Yes! Exactly, but we will most likely stay here for the time being. Luckily we won't have to wake up to a counter-attack or an ambush." A smile peeking through Winston's dirt covered face, his teeth bright white, whiter from the off tone of the dirt.

The roaring sound of tanks and trucks signaled the rest of the men to run towards them cheering and holding their helmets up in the air. I stayed by Winston as we waited for the relief force to enter the square. Looking down the street, my eyes caught the first glimpse of a Sherman tank. A beastly vehicle that could take a hit and still push forward. The low rumble then became deafening to my ears. Ten of them came down the road, shaking rocks and dirt off rubble piles and making my stomach blend together. On each side of the tank column a line of men marching, each man hard faced and hollow.

"Where is your superior officer? I need to talk to him about further operations in this area." A middle age man with dark brown eyes and black hair with silver streaks running through it asked Winston, the officer's eyes never leaving his.

"He's over by the front of the church." Pointing behind him towards the church with his thumb.

"Thank you, son. How did you hold up here?"

"Our initial attack was a success, heavy casualties, but manageable. We intercepted the retreating forces and captured around fifty. It's great to finally get relief, sir."

"You boys go relax, we will stick around till noon and then continue our advance towards Paris." The officer told us, walking past and giving me a pat on the back.

"Warren, you should go wash up by the creek. That's going to be where everyone else will be. I'm going to be with Captain to understand what our next plan is." Winston told me. I started walking back to the eastern part of the village where Gold Company was staying. Not a single building was unscathed from the impacts of war.

The streets alone had an eerie feeling to it, even though there was no threat around.

The outskirts of the village were different than the heart of it, green pastures and trees standing strong with their leaves blowing against the soft, cool breeze. The one bridge that Gold was supposed to defend still stood. Two soldiers were climbing around it disarming the devices that they planted there the night we captured the village. The sky was clear, and the sun was at its highest point shining down on the land. When I reached the water, I saw that other guys had the same idea. Before my body could bend down controllably, my legs gave out, and I collapsed to the ground. The water of the creek was crystal clear, my reflection was resembling that of a mirror. Looking at my reflection, I noticed that my face was caked with dirt and blood, but not my blood, and I didn't know whose it was. *It was probably the German that almost killed me last night.* The hollowness in my eyes looked dark and filled with events that they wanted to erase, not the light blue that held the innocence of my youth. The water was cool and refreshing when I dunked my head under the surface, my hands running over my face to wash off the dirt and dried blood. The essence of war running off into the creek which may lead to another village or town that will then see the horrors.

Walking back to the house that my company was staying in, I could feel the atmosphere was different in the surrounding streets. Men were talking, laughing, and for the first time in a while, smiles were being passed around.

Tommy, a young boy from Pittsburgh with hazel eyes, brown hair with blonde streaks running through, and a little scrawny found a working piano from one of the undamaged houses and brought it out into the square where a group surrounded him singing along with the tune. It appeared the war ended, and we were celebrating our contribution, but that was not the case. We were unwinding from all the stress and relaxing our nerves.

The house I was staying in was small but big enough for twenty guys to sleep and relax comfortably inside. To help unwind more, ranking officers and privates could room together. Of course, Winston and I shared a room together, no bigger than the tent we shared in England. Two queen size beds, a shelve used to put our ammo bags, helmets, and other personal material. A wooden desk placed closer to the door was where Winston stayed most of the mid-afternoon typing out death reports from the previous battles which will be sent to high command and then handed to random men who will tell mothers, wives, fathers, or whoever that their family member was killed in battle and died heroically. The scene of him typing these sent shivers up my spine and knots in my stomach. I didn't want to imagine him typing out one with my name and cause of death.

"How many do you have to type?" I asked him while sitting on the bed looking towards his bent back which gave the signs of stress and tiredness.

"One hundred and twenty. We lost about sixty percent of our company in forty-eight hours. I still have seventy-two to go." His hands covered his face as a heavy sigh passed through. "Captain says we are staying here for three more days to resupply and get fresh troops. After that, we are supposed to push north and secure the area north of Paris for the main force to keep pushing forward. I don't want to imagine how bad the men on the beach landing had it. This war will destroy everything and no one on Earth will be untouched by it."

No words could come out of my mouth. I could only just sit on the bed that didn't feel soft anymore as Winston continued with his reports, his face was full of gloom and disbelief and sadness. Throwing my feet onto the bed, I looked up at the ceiling thinking of the events that have already accrued. The screams and gunfire becoming intense again.

"Warren take cover!" An explosion went off yards away from me as we kept running across the field to the next cow corpse. "Move up! Keep

pushing!" The voice of Lee coming through the scene. Then it changed to inside the village, where a man was screaming for his mom, and the medic was trying to stop the blood pouring out of the massive hole in his stomach from a grenade blast.

"Warren, you ok?" Reality came back, and my eyes locked onto Winston who was standing over me with a concerned look on his face. "You were talking in your sleep. Something about grabbing more bandages for some guy."

"Yeah, just a nightmare. You're done with the reports?"

"No, I still have thirty to go. If I get done soon enough, you want to go downstairs and play poker with some of the guys?"

"That sounds like fun, better work on those reports, so I can take all your smokes," I said with a laughing manner behind the words. Even though poker was not my game, I still had a pretty good poker face to fool even the best player in Gold. Winston returned to his typewriter and sat down on the wooden chair he borrowed from the dining room. I sat up and thought about my dream and how these will never leave me. Getting up from the bed I walked over to the shelf where my notepad was and grabbed a pencil as well.

It's been too long since I wrote home. Maybe since we control a part of France, we can start to get mail shipments in and receive some letters my mom sent me during the time we left England. Saying in my head as the pencil started to create words on the paper that would express all my pent-up emotions.

Dear Mother,

It has been some time since I have written to you. We are in Lisieux, a tiny little village that is a few miles inland. You would like it, with all the bakeries and small shops. I would like to come back one day and see this place not devastated by war and take you with as well. Winston is still alive, and we are both unscathed. I know keeping Dale away from the news will be hard, but just keep him informed that I'm still alive and will come home one day. I won't get into the gruesome part of the war, but it does change a man's thoughts. We will be taking Paris in a few weeks, I cannot wait to see the Eiffel Tower when we get there. Luckily Gold Company is ordered to rest for the next few days, and then we must secure the area north of Paris. I love you mom and tell Dale I love him as well.

Hopefully, I'll be back before Christmas, but a part of me doesn't see that happening.

Love always,

Your son, Joseph.

"Warren, you ready to lose at poker?" Winston said getting up from his desk, pushing the chair in.

"You mean to win." Standing up and tossing the letter and pencil to the bed. We both walked out of the room and down the stairs to a smoke-filled dining room where three other soldiers were sitting around a wooden table with cards and packs of cigarettes talking about how they will lose the game or how Hitler is wetting his pants right now.

"Got the room for two more?" Winston chimed in patting me on the back with a smile.

"Sure do, just grab some seats, and we will deal you in. Got smokes to wager with?" A man spoke with a large cigar in his mouth, his face was chiseled out of solid granite, and his eyes were a demonic black with a twisted smile.

"I think he's a cheater," I whispered over to Winston as we grabbed two chairs and sat around the table.

Winston replied with a glance and said, "If he is what do we have to lose? A pack of smokes."

We both tossed in one pack, I didn't care if all the rounds would be a loss because smoking was never a thing that caught my attention. I quickly glanced over at Winston who looked at his hand and gave a faint smirk. Either his hand was good, or the smile was to throw people off from how bad it was. I had no clue what my hand was, as this was my first time ever playing poker.

"Well, gentlemen, I'm out." A man across the table from me threw in his cards and walked away. That only left the guy sitting next to Winston, the supposed cheater, and me.

"Yeah same here guys." The man sitting next to Winston said standing up and tossing his cards into the pile.

"In that case, I'll toss in two more packs. Make things interesting." The man with the cigar said as he took it out of his mouth and released a large cloud of smoke which lingered over the table.

"So, pal, what's your name. I haven't gotten a chance to see everyone from Gold since training." Winston said tossing in another pack after looking at his hand.

"Charlie, Charlie Keller from Indianapolis. I signed up because my brother volunteered before Pearl Harbor and died there from one of the bomb explosions." Charlie looked down to the table and fixed on a small cut on it where his finger ran over the trench repeatedly.

"I'm sorry for your loss. You're doing your brother proud." Winston told Charlie, placing a hand on his shoulder to show him that he cared.

"Thank you. Now back this game." Charlie took a puff of his cigar and looked hard at his cards. "Warren, right? Either you don't know how to play poker, or you have the world's best poker face."

"I've played a little back home." The words were oozing in between my teeth, looking at what I assumed was a bad hand. "But, I'm out." Dropping my cards to the table surface.

Winston's face went from calm to confusion, so did Charlie's, his cigar almost dropping out of his mouth. "What?" Both men said in sync, making me wonder how great my hand was.

"You really don't know how to play poker Warren," Winston said while releasing a laugh that caused Charlie to join in. "You would have won."

"Yeah, I know I can't play, but you two can divvy up the pile of smokes," I told them while standing up and pushing in the chair. Giving a smile to Winston and a nod to Charlie. I exited the living room and proceeded back to my room where I could finally finish the book I started back in England.

Chapter VI

Skirmish

Today was the first week of August, and our company was given more time for rest due to the supply line running behind, but when the supplies and reinforcements came, they brought up fresh troops and ammo. Our company was given one hundred and fifty men, bringing our company's total to two hundred and ten men.

"Do you know when the mail line will be connected?" I asked Winston walking side by side to the church where Captain was about to tell us new orders on the task that was given.

"No, I don't. I'll ask Captain after the speech." Winston looked at me knowing that I wanted to know if my mom ever wrote back and that the feeling of her knowing I'm still alive was building inside of me.

"Hopefully when we capture Paris our company could stay there for a few days." Jokingly punching me in the arm. Both of us smiled as we reached the church where most of Gold Company was already waiting for what was next. "I'll see you after the speech, maybe another game of poker?"

"Maybe." A smile fell through as Winston walked up to the foot of the church steps to prepare the men for Captain's arrival. I fell in line and waiting like everyone else.

"Attention!" Winston's voice forcing everyone to become silent and stood at attention with legs spread a foot apart and hands behind their back.

Captain proceeded to walk up the steps to be in full view for everyone, "At ease gentlemen. You are all gathered here today to be informed of our next mission. After the three days of rest and weeks of standby, resupply of ammo, and fresh troops, high command has seen it fit for us to move out. The main force has been pushing back the Germans for the past three weeks and is about four days west of Paris. Our mission is to secure the northern sector, so no German counter-attack can halt the attack on Paris. Once we take Paris, the German army will be fiercer and fight harder, knowing that the next key location is the Rhine River which separates Germany and France. Most of you haven't experienced combat yet, some of you have sacrificed more than I could ask for, but we will all be prepared for this mission. Dismissed." Captain walked down the stairs towards Winston who was being informed of the mission. Both soldiers saluted and went their separate paths.

"Captain told me that we are moving out in two hours. So, pack up and get ready to move." Winston informed me as we regrouped while everyone else was walking back to whatever they were doing before.

"I'm assuming we will be walking." My comment sounding more displeased than I wanted to be.

"Yeah, but it shouldn't be that bad. It's a nice day out, and Paris is one hundred and five miles away, so we will be a day behind the main force. If we are lucky, the Germans won't put that much of a fight for the city, and we can capture it with ease."

"Guess we'll find out when the day comes." Opening the door to the house where our gear was. The house and this village will forever stay in my memories. The men that died here will be close to my heart and will never be forgotten because without them this invasion would not be successful.

The two hours before moving out was calm, no one was running around, and the air was silent and peaceful. My gear was neatly placed on the shelf untouched with my rifle leaning against it and my helmet sitting on top of my rifle's barrel.

"*Will what comes next to be worse than this?*" I was afraid of what the Germans had in store for defense, but we had to go forward no matter the cost.

"Warren, we are moving out!" Winston said running up the stairs in all gear with his Thompson slung over his shoulder. His face calm and his eyes wide for the unknown that will come.

"Okay, hopefully, you're right about the German's not really defending Paris. I would like to see the Eiffel Tower, not destroyed." Laughing while finishing my comment to him.

"Same here man. Captain wants us to form up by the bridge. I'll wait for you outside." Walking down the stairs and the door creaked open then slammed shut. I checked my rifle to see if it was fully loaded and then ran down the steps and flew outside the door almost running into Winston who was waiting a few feet away from the door.

"Someone is eager." He laughed as we started walking towards the bridge.

The sky was a refreshing blue, with the sun beaming down on the French countryside. There was no breeze, but the humidity was not bad, and for being in a village torn apart by war, there was no other sign of it in the surrounding areas. The men who came in with the supply line were eager to get their chance to kill Germans, but the men who I jumped into France with just stood around, not talking about killing or the war in general. They instead were talking about home, their wives or girlfriends, and what their small town looked like.

"Form up boys!" Captain yelled by standing on the bridge trying to get everyone's attention. After everyone heard the command, we got into two lines. One on each side of the road with Captain in the lead of the line on the left side and Winston in the lead on the right side. I was right behind Charlie who was third in line on the left side. "Move out!" Captain ordered, and in sync, we all started marching to somewhere north of Paris.

The French countryside looked something out of a painting. The rolling hills and the never ending green pastures with aqua blue skies and large clouds so pure that they almost looked like something from a dream. Then there were the horrors of war that tarnished the beauty of the scene.

Burnt out tanks, destroyed trucks, and cars, and dead horses and ox corpses bloated on the sides of the road. My nostrils were on fire from the horrible smells of decomposing bodies and burning metal. War was inescapable even when surrounded by a beautiful landscape.

The sun was casting an orange and purple haze over the retreating afternoon sky from the advancing evening glow. We have been marching for about ten hours and got forty miles in before we stopped to sleep the night. Shadows grew as the last remnants of the evening sun withdrew behind the cover of a hillside. With that, night fell upon us, and everything seemed more peaceful except the constant distant booming of artillery guns and the flashes of explosions lighting up the sky in the horizon.

"Gold Company set up camp alongside the road in the ditch. We will continue moving at first light." Captain gave the order as all two hundred and ten men walked off the road and dropped into the rain ditch right beside the road.

"Hey, Winston. Where are we even going? I know our destination is north of Paris, but are we going to a town or just an empty field?

"Captain said we are going to the town of Asnières. It's about the size of Lisieux, but no garrison, because all the suburban towns' garrisons have been relocated to Paris. We are only going there to secure a bridge and repel any German counterattack that might happen." He said as we both got into a somewhat comfortable position before laying down and watched the stars' dance among the dead of night, while faint echoes of explosions and fighting lurked in the distance. A clear reminder that war will never stop.

"At this rate, we might be home before Christmas," I said putting both my arms behind my head as my eyes locked their gaze on a set of stars dangling next to the crescent moon.

"That or by New Years, but either way I don't see this war lasting any longer than a year. Hitler screwed himself over when he invaded Russia, and even if he does have an ace or two up his sleeve, he will still lose this war." Shuffling around to get a more reasonable position before closing his eyes and waiting for the next day of marching to come upon us. I did the same as well and closed my eyes hoping nothing will ruin the easy march and capture of a town.

"*German tanks take cover! Warren on me, Winston take Bravo squad and flank around them! Hold this bridge at all costs!*"

"Rise and shine Gold Company! We have a long day's march ahead of us, and we don't want to be late for the party now do we?" Captain said over the rustle of men getting up or finishing getting all their gear together.

I opened my eyes welcoming the warmth of the sun to overtake me and help wake up from what I thought was a reality. The morning dew soaked my back, and a few grass blades hung to the shirt. My gear was already packed probably by Winston earlier in the morning. There was a fire going on in the field beside the road where a few men were cooking eggs that were most likely stolen from a nearby farm. Chatter was filling the void with anticipation and homesickness. There wasn't any artillery fire happening in the distance, but rather clouds of thick smoke rose to the heavens in multiple directions.

After today we should be able to reach
Asnières by mid-morning tomorrow. That is if we don't
meet any resistance on the way.

"Warren, Joseph Warren!" A clean faced private said to me coming over in a brand-new uniform unscathed by war.

"I'm over here." Notifying the boy with the waving of my hand. As he got closer, I asked, "What is it?"

"Captain wants a talk with you. He's over by the burnt-out truck."

"Okay, thank you." I got up and grabbed my rifle placing the sling over my shoulder. My helmet locked in between my hip and my arm. Then proceeded down the road for ten yards to hear what Captain wants to tell me.

"Sir, Private Joseph H. Warren reporting for duty." I barked out my presence as my right arm rose to a saluting stance.

"At ease son. I wanted to talk to you about a special request." He said to me unrolling a map of the area onto the warped metal hood of the truck.

"I would do whatever you want me to, sir." My chest started to get tighter as the fears of what was to come next flooded my imagination. *What does he want me to do? I'm still only a private.*

"Good to hear that, because I want you, Lieutenant Jones, and three other men to go out ahead of the rest of the company and scout the area. Get to about five miles from the targeted town and wait for us to arrive." His voice was calm and understanding if I were to say no. "If you meet any enemy units do not engage and pull back to inform me. Intel reports that there shouldn't be any units this far north of Paris as our main forces are moving in on the French capital, but we shouldn't let our guard down. Will you accept this request?" His eyes searching in mine for an answer that wouldn't displease him.

"Of course, sir. Lieutenant Jones and I will gather three other men and move out in thirty minutes." The words slipping through my lips faster than I could catch them. The knot in my stomach grew tighter, fear drew pictures of hidden Germans ready to plunge a dagger into my back or an MG42 opening fire out of some brushes cutting my body in half.

"Good, Lieutenant Jones is by the fire talking to some lads. Seeing if they want to join the scouting party."

"Thank you, sir." I raised my arm again to salute, Captain saluted in return, and I turned to walk towards Winston with fear running all around my body.

"Oh, Warren. By the way, you are an excellent soldier. I'll keep you in mind for a medal or two by the end of the war." Captain said to me as I was halfway down the ditch.

"Thank you, sir." A calming sensation eased the fear and fried nerves. I continued my walk towards the fire where I could see Winston patting a guy on the back who was sitting eating an egg out of his tin cup. "Lieutenant Jones, ready to move out?" Walking up to him and looking at the three men sitting around the fire eating their breakfast.

"Yeah, these three guys are willing to go with us." Winston turned to reply to me as the three other men stood up quickly and got into attention. They were new soldiers by the way they reacted without knowing I was only a private.

"Private Bryce Taylor." The one shorter man said as he started to salute me. He had dark brown hair with chocolate colored eyes. He had stubble that looked more like a never leaving shadow.

"Guys, I'm only a private as well. The only man you will be saluting in this squad is Lieutenant Jones." I told the three men now looking embarrassed as Winston and I both started to laugh. "But I would like to know all your names before we go."

"Private Jacob Lewis." He said with helmet perfectly tightened and his rifle slung over his shoulder. His hair was a dirty blonde with little slivers peeking out from the crease of the helmet, and his eyes were of a gemstone blue.

The last guy was built, I supposed he worked in a factory on the east coast. He was an older man, in his mid-twenties with black hair and hazel eyes. "Private Jose Ramirez."

"I'm Joseph Warren. Captain told Jones and me that we will be scouting the area till we reach Asnières. If we meet any Germans, we are not allowed to engage them. We are ordered to fall back and regroup with the company."

They all understood as Winston, and I walked up to the road with them following behind, eager to maybe see some action. I just wanted to survive another day and hopefully, see the end of this war. We all checked our ammo and racked our rifles to make sure a bullet was on standby just in case we had to shoot.

"Okay, let's move out," Winston told us as we started walking down the road in a line either towards death or a silent town. The sun was high over our shoulders, and the air was sweet with the blooming of summer field flowers. It was a peaceful countryside, and this scared me. It made me think that we were not in for an easy mission, that this may be the last time the landscape will look beautiful just like it seemed back in England.

Hours passed since we left the company behind for the town of Asnières. The road went from pavement to dirt, and the soft fields turned to thick, endless forests on both sides of the road. The only sounds that I could hear were that of birds singing and leaves rustling in the warm summer breeze. Winston was in the lead with me right behind, and Jacob, Jose, and Bryce filled up the rear. We all had our rifles unslung and pointed to the ground. Everyone was on edge and waited for the ripping of a machine gun or the crack of a sniper rifle, but neither came to sound.

Winston raised a fist in the air and kneeled to the ground. We all knelt as well and kept quiet.

Does he hear something? Does he see something? The questions raced through my mind as we waited for our next order. Winston turned around, took his hand and motioned us to move into the cover of the forest with his lips forming the word "quickly" as well.

Our squad ducked into the darkness of the forest confused and concerned. I looked over as Winston who turned his head to face me and raised a finger to his mouth.

"What did you hear?" I motioned with my mouth still confused on what's happening. But I realized all was quiet, the soft whistling of the birds had ceased, and the warm breeze was no longer there.

"Tank engines," Winston replied by mouthing the words. That sent my blood ice cold, and daggers pierced my stomach.

It's possible that the engines could be friendly, but who would be this far northeast behind the mainline?

We hunkered down as the earth started to vibrate under our feet. The vibration felt as though my insides were being blended together and turned to liquid. My face was inches from the ground to conceal myself the best, and the dirt was sifting away from my body. We could hear the deafening engines roar louder as they drove closer and closer to us, the mechanical squeal of massive wheels moving inside the treds. I was too afraid to look up from the dirt, my heart was racing and my breathing heavy as it was, I tried to keep quiet and calm. My left hand gripping my rifle tighter as my right pressed hard on my helmet.

Then the sounds stopped, and all was quiet. I lifted my head a few inches and looked over my right shoulder to see Jacob raise his body a little to see what was going on.

"Jacob, get down." Winston quietly ordered still hunkered down on the cool, wet ground. Bryce tried to grab his pants, but Jacob was already crawling towards the road out from the cover of the forest.

Looking over to Winston my face was high in concern, not for Jacob, but for all of us. Winston knew exactly what I was showing and feeling. With that, he motioned with his hands to stay low and move deeper into the forest to stay concealed. Jose and Bryce went first as Winston, and I stayed back to cover any possible enemy encounter. None of us knew whose tanks that we felt and heard come down the road until the blood-curdling sound of an MG34 opened fire. The yelling of German voices forced me to shoot up and run deeper into the forest. Winston and the other two were right on my tail as we didn't want to get caught by the bullets of a German machine gun.

Don't look back, don't look back. I kept telling myself over and over as the voices of the enemy decreased in volume and then were overpowered by the crunching and snapping of forest vegetation mixed in with the sounds of heavy breathing and loose pocket items bouncing around.

"Take defensive positions till all clear," Winston said sliding behind a fallen tree and raising his rifle to shoot the first movement he sees. Jose took position next to him, and Bryce took his behind a large boulder. I slipped behind a thin pine tree and steadied my hands, so my accuracy wouldn't be horrible.

"Jacob is dead, isn't he?" Jose said placing the front end of his rifle against the fallen tree to steady his aim.

"Obviously, man didn't you hear the machine gun. He's probably cut in half in the middle of the road." Bryce said with fear radiating off his words.

"Both of you calm down. Yes, Private Lewis is dead and will be missed, but his death will not go in vain. We must get back to Gold Company and tell

Captain that there is a tank column moving down the road." Winston tried to pour confidence in Jose's eyes and then turned to look at Bryce.

"We will get through this." I gave them both one last comforting remark before we waited five minutes for any movement and then made our way back to the company.

It was late afternoon till everyone's nerves were calmed down and we covered around two miles from where the German tank column was. The sun was poking through small pockets of clearing to illuminate the ground of the forest. The air turned cool, and a light breeze handed us fresh air to relax with while blowing the tops of the knee-high grass. There were no sounds of war anywhere around us. *I've seen so much death in just a month, but this is war and death is a guarantee in war.*

"So, Warren where are you from?" With the question releasing from Bryce's lips a crack from a rifle rings through the forest, forcing us to drop to the forest floor.

"Everyone alright!" I screamed, more concerned that Winston was hit instead of myself or the other two men.

"Where the hell did that come from?" Jose asked clutching the ground around him making no movement to ensure the sniper wouldn't pick him off next.

"Sound off!" Winston ordered to make sure everyone was still alive and that we didn't lose a second person today. One by one we all sounded off until Bryce sounded off and he sounded different.

"Bryce, are you okay?" I asked not moving an inch

"I'm fine, I think I landed on a rock when falling."

"Does anyone know where that came from?" Winston asked trying to figure out a way to get all of us out of here alive.

"I think it came from behind us, from the way it sounded," Jose said trying to hold back tears of fear.

I was lying a few feet from him whispering "We will make it out alive." Showing him that no one else must die today from our squad.

"Lieutenant Jones, I have an idea. I'm going to raise my helmet a few inches and see where the bullet comes from." Saying with a soft voice as I slowly took my helmet off exposing my easy penetrable skull.

"Okay, once the helmet is hit, we will know the general direction of the sniper and throw two smoke grenades to cover our retreat," Winston said getting a smoke grenade out of his front pocket and prepared to pull the pin.

Looking closely at my helmet the details seemed clearer. The dark olive-green paint covering the steel helmet with dirt covering some parts and blood covering others. Chips of the paint were scraped off from shrapnel and debris. I lifted it slowly waiting for the harsh impact of a German bullet.

Tightening my grip on the side of my helmet and slowly raised it so our decoy could be visible above the knee-high grass that gave us cover from instant death. I must have raised it only a few inches above the grass before the impact of the bullet ripped it out of my hands snapping my wrist back and sending the helmet tumble down next to me. The crack of the rifle echoed throughout the forest and signified that our hunter was still waiting for someone to peek up and die. My helmet had a small hole in the front and a bigger size one coming out from the back.

"Our sniper is behind us. All of us should throw a smoke grenade to make a larger wall of cover," I informed the rest of my squad as my hand felt for the smooth metal cylinder of a smoke grenade held inside my back pocket.

"On my mark then," Winston said waiting for everyone to equip a smoke grenade. "Mark." The clicking of the grenade's pin being released as all four of us tossed them towards the sniper's area. The cans started to sizzle as the smoke billowed out while in mid-air. "Count to three and then run."

*One...*My breathing became heavy, and my heart started to race....*Two...*I gripped my rifle tighter and placed my helmet back onto my head even with a hole going right through the center. The smoke creating a large cloud that looked more like highly dense fog....*Three...*I shot up and bolted through the forest, jumping over fallen logs and ducking under low-hanging branches. A shot went off, most likely from the sniper taking a guess. *Don't look back.* I could see an opening and a woodshed standing alone at the edge of the forest about two hundred yards away.

"Keep running! Take cover behind that shed!" Winston was yelling, running past Jose and Bryce who were right behind me. Two gunshots went off as Jose stopped running, turned and knelt to steady his covering fire. "Jose, just keep moving!"

My lungs were on fire as sweat started to trickle down my face, the forest became less dense, and the sun started to shine brighter at the end of the forest getting closer and closer. "*Just keep moving.*" My mind was screaming at my body to not stop. "*If you stop, you will die.*" The shed was a hundred yards away. It was a small, simple woodshed that loggers used to store wood for the winter. It was the only structure in the whole area except for stone walls and a few burnt-out vehicles.

The shed was now fifty yards and another crack from a gunshot. "The sniper is just shooting random. Just keep moving." Yelling to the rest of my squad never turning my head, only focusing on the shed. Breathing became hard, my heart demanded more room to pump, and my legs screamed for relaxation.

I finally reached the shed and rounded the corner, sliding behind the back wall and trying to relax while steadying my heart rate and breathing. Winston and Jose rounded the corner right after me and collapsed to the ground. Bryce was the last one to come around and dropped quickly once he knew he was behind the safety of cover.

"Everyone okay?" I said sitting up against the shed catching my breath from the hard run.

"I'm good." Jose and Winston said in unison, both still lying on the ground with their chests rising and falling quickly.

"Bryce, are you-" My voice silenced, and a rush of energy swarmed through my body. "Winston, Bryce got hit." Calling out as I crawled over to Bryce who was clutching his side and pain radiating off his face.

"I don't think that was a rock I landed on back there," Bryce said jokingly showing a glimpse of humor during a time of fear.

"Does anyone have bandages or anything?" Concern leaked in with my words, trying to keep my calm and not wanting to lose another soldier who was too young to die.

Bryce let out a loud, painful scream as blood kept oozing out of his side and soaked into his shirt leaving a massive stain. "Warren, tell my mom I'm sorry." He grabbed my hand and placed it on his side to put pressure down, hopefully, to stop or slow down the bleeding.

"No, don't say that. You are going to survive and get to go home." I told Bryce as my hands tried to keep the pressure on the wound. "You are going to live." As the words left my mouth the grip of Bryce's hand relaxed and his eyes started to fade into an endless stare.

The sun's rays were hidden by the incoming clouds with the breeze quickening. Droplets of rain danced off our helmets and the roof of the shed with each passing second the intensity grew. My grip on Bryce's hand never relaxed till Winston reached down and grabbed his dog tag while placing a hand on my shoulder.

"We need to go Warren," Winston said standing back up.

Why did it have to be him? My mind demanding answers on why he was the next to die and not me, or someone else.

"Warren!" Winston's voice came through and brought me back to reality. The rain was pouring, and the only sounds were that of water hitting metal and falling off leaves into the nearby forest floor. I released Bryce's hand letting his empty body rest against a woodshed in the middle of a French field a thousand miles away from his home.

"Goodbye Private Bryce Taylor, it was an honor serving with you," I said in a soft voice almost a whisper, giving a final salute. Then I turned around and walked up to Winston and Jose who were waiting for me.

The trek back to the area where Gold Company was hard, the rain turned the road into a muddy swamp, and the fields acted as glue. After two more hours of walking, we finally reached Gold Company who took camp inside a wooded area off the road to take cover from the rain. All three of us were tired and exhausted from the march, but also emotionally tired from the fighting and death that happened. My mind was still stuck on the death of Bryce and the sound of the machine gun that tore through Jacob. It has been a little over two months since the invasion, and this war has completely drained me of emotions.

When we reached our company, Jose walked towards a small group of soldiers who were all hunkering under a single blanket.

They look new, maybe he knows them, I said in my head walking with Winston to where Captain was sitting with a map covered in plastic to not get ruined by the rain.

"Sir, scouting party has returned with some news," Winston announced standing in front of Captain who looked up with a nervous, but anxious expression.

"Go ahead, Lieutenant." Captain said folding up the map and placing it in one of his inside coat pockets.

"We were eight miles from the town when we encountered a German tank column. We took cover before they saw us, but Private Jacob Lewis went out of cover and was killed. After that, we were ambushed by a sniper where Private Bryce Taylor was shot. We were able to cover our run with the help of Private Joseph Warren and reached a woodshed on the outskirts of the forest where Private Taylor died from his wound. Private Jose Ramirez was unscathed and helped cover our run from the sniper by providing cover fire. I suspect that the tank column was heading towards Paris so our march to Asnières will be smooth." Winston told Captain all in a matter of two minutes. I was trying to hold back tears when he was talking about the death of Jacob and Bryce, but I knew that crying over everyone that died would become more tiring than marching for twenty-four hours.

"Thank you for the information Lieutenant, you are dismissed. Private Warren can I have a word with you?" Captain said as the rain started to ease off and the sun started to peek through a little.

"Yes, Captain?" Asking in a curious tone, but still showed confidence and steadiness.

"With your actions taken today, I want to recognize you for the Bronze Star." He said with a smile on his face, extending a hand out to me in a kind gesture.

"Sir, permission to speak freely?"

"Permission granted Private." retracting his hand and stood up.

"Sir, with all due respect and honor for this recognition, I do not feel obligated to receive it. Yes, I helped get the squad away from the sniper, but Private Taylor still died in the process. Therefore I do not feel that the medal should be awarded to me."

"I respect your opinion and won't send a letter back to higher command then. What you did out there though was brave, and I thank you for saving most of your squad."

"Thank you, sir," I said saluting him. After he saluted in return, I turned away and walked to where Winston was sitting, head in between his legs.

"Are you okay?" Sitting down next to him and placing my hands on my knees.

He raised his head, tears rolled down his cheeks, "I lost two men who never saw combat before today. Now I must write two more letters to two different mothers saying how honorable their son died. Honestly Warren, I just want this damn war to be over."

"It almost is. We are about to take Paris, and once we push the Germans out of France they will be fighting in Germany, plus they are getting stomped on against the Russians so this war might be over in a few months." Trying to say anything that would make him calm down from his sadness. "Hey, I heard that French women *love* American men," I said with a smirk, and instantly Winston picked up his head, and the crying stopped.

"Really?" Wiping away his tears and looking at me. His eyes instead of showing sadness and remorse now show excitement and joy.

"Yeah, I also heard that they also like Americans who are high ranking like yourself." Knowing the plan is working I stood up and helped Winston up as well.

"We better take Paris quick then. Or all the ladies will run away." Winston started to laugh as he stood up and joined me to gather the rest of the company to finish the march.

I fell in line behind Winston while him,
Lieutenant. Thomas and Captain go over the battle
plan, "We only have five more hours till we reach our
objective. Once we get there, I want to split into three
teams to secure all parts of Asnières and the two
bridges that lead to Paris. Winston, I want you to take
Alpha Team, I'll take Bravo, and Lieutenant Thomas will
take Charlie. Alpha and Charlie will secure the two
bridges while Bravo will secure the town's square.
Everyone understand?" Both Winston and Thomas
agreed to the operation that will unfold later this
evening. "Okay good, let's move out."

Chapter VII

The Horrors of War

Once again, we marched towards our goal, I was already tired from the scouting march earlier today, my muscles screaming for rest, and ached for something to help get them relaxed. All my gear felt heavier than usual, but that was due to the fatigue that started to set in. Morale throughout the company was still high. Seeing no combat, the past two months helped everyone, by giving us time to write some letters back to home and receive some as well. Last week we got a mail truck, and everyone including me was anxious to get a letter from home, but I did not receive anything. Winston got a short letter from his mom telling him that she is proud of him and that everyone in his town has been praying for his safe return.

The five-hour march went by quick. We didn't meet any resistance, and the tank column that we encountered earlier was nowhere to be found. We took a different road to reach the town, and my heart stopped for a second knowing that I will never see the two men ever again.

"Everyone halt!" Captain's voice rang out over the quietness of the evening. I could feel my stomach start to tighten as the unknowing events that were about to happen.

Maybe there are snipers, or maybe they booby trapped every other block. My mind started to race with questions, images of bodies ripped apart and sounds of explosions filled my imagination.

Captain then grabbed Winston and Thomas to start the advance into the town.

"Bravo Team, which is the first half of the right column follow me!" Winston's voice booming with no hint of concern or nervousness. Rushing over to where Winston was waiting, myself and seventy men gathered around to hear what our objective would be to secure the town. "Our team is tasked with securing one of the bridges leading towards Paris. We must defend the bridge at all costs without destroying it. Be swift, but also stay alert, we don't know if there is still resistance or if they planted traps to slow our advance. Good luck."

Our advance was slow, no one wanted to take the chance and walk out of cover to be met by a sniper's bullet. At every intersection, Winston checked the ground for trip wires or anything that would set off a booby trap. The bridge was two blocks away, but in between us and the bridge were perfect places for a machine gun nest or hiding spots for German snipers to pick us off one by one.

Winston halted our slow walk and ordered us to press our bodies against the wall of a shop that we were walking by before crossing the first block, "Warren, you and Private Ramirez go investigate the house right there." Pointing to a two-story row home. All the windows were blown out, and the door was closed. The stonework that covered the outside was caked in a dark powder, most likely from a past fire.

Shaking my head in acceptance, I looked back at Jose to see if he was ready. His eyes were hard, and his hands could barely hold up the rifle. He was scared, he already saw two men get killed today without ever firing a shot. Taking a deep breath Jose and I started to move slowly to the edge of the building where we prepared ourselves for the sprint across the street.

I looked over at Jose who was trying to keep calm, but clearly showed he was nervous. I placed a hand on his shoulder, "Hey, it's going to be okay. It is just a quick sprint, and there is a good chance that there are no snipers or anything."

His body resided from its tense state and became more relaxed. "Okay, let's do this." The grip on his rifle became normal, his eyes focused and alert. We waited a few seconds before I gave the signal to him.

"On three, one...two...three." We turned the corner at high speed and never stopped running.

No sniper, no machine gun. So far so good. Comforting myself as I threw my body into the door of a two-story house, breaking it open with a loud thud. Jose was right behind me and ran right into the house, rifle up ready to shoot down any German who made a defensive position inside. Panning from left to right we cleared the first floor. The house was small and full of dusty furniture untouched since the family left. The living room only held a sofa, and a coffee table, with a side table against a wall and a radio standing on it covered in an inch of dust. The kitchen was minuscule as well with a wood burning stove and a sink that was flooded with dirty dishes.

Placing my rifle up on my shoulder, finger resting on the trigger and my cheek getting warm from sitting on the polished wood of my rifle. I motioned to Jose that we should check the second floor now.

"I'll take the point." He said walking in front of me standing at the bottom of the stairs, rifle aimed at the top.

"Okay, I'll be right behind you. If there was someone here, they would have shot at us by now." Standing right behind him as we inched our way up the stairs. My heart was pounding, and sweat started to trickle down my forehead, not knowing if we were alone or if some German was waiting upstairs ready to kill the first American to walk upstairs.

Be calm, just like you said there probably isn't anyone here.

The creaking of the stairs did not help relax my heart rate, and with Jose taking point I didn't want to see another friend get killed. Everything was perfectly quiet except the stairs screaming underneath the pressure of our feet. Before my foot could be planted on the ground, I heard a soft crack of wood from a footstep. My blood went cold, and my body grew heavy, there was a third person in this house.

"Jose!" Before he could turn around a German came around the corner and shot multiple rounds into Jose's stomach. My finger pressed hard on the trigger, the loud burst of the gunshot rattled my eardrums. Jose's body fell into me forcing both of us to fall to the bottom the stairs, but before I fell to the first floor, my eyes caught a glimpse of the German's body drop to the ground, blood splattered against the wall. Jose's body was heavier than I first realized and luckily, I sustained no injuries. Thanks to my helmet, my head did not get slammed against the wooden steps.

"Are you guys okay?" Winston and two other soldiers came running through the door to see what the gunfire was. Winston ran over to where I laid with Jose's body lying next to me face down as the two other soldiers ran up the stairs to secure the second floor. "Warren, are you okay? What happened?" His voice was filled with concern and surprise.

"Yeah, I'm-" My words were cut off by the crack of a rifle, my eyes shot up to the top of the stairs, where the two soldiers stood, one bringing down his rifle as the other one gave the signal for all clear. "I'm fine, I don't think Private Ramirez is though." My voice trembled through the still shaken experience that almost lead to my death. The two soldiers walking down the stairs now picking up Jose's body and moving it outside where once we secure the town a medic truck would be called up and take his body back to the rear.

Winston helped me up and reached down to pick up my rifle. "I heard a sound when we were walking up the stairs, I shouldn't have yelled his name. Winston, I'm sorry." My voice cracked as guilt infiltrated my mind and swelled in my eyes creating tears of sorrow.

"It's not your fault. There was no way to control the situation. You did all you could, Jose would be proud that you tried to protect him." His voice was soft and comforting, almost like a father talking to his son after a lost baseball game. Most of the guilt drained from my mind and calmness eased its way back in. "We are only a block away from the bridge, once we set up a defensive position there I'll let you sit back and help me figure out any fallback maneuvers if we get overwhelmed."

"I'll be okay but thank you." Grabbing my rifle as Winston handed it over, I exited the house and proceeded to where the rest of Bravo Team was waiting for the signal to advance. My mind still trying to absorb all the death and destruction that has laid wake so far. The ringing in my ears was the clear reminder that Jose was killed, but I wasn't.

Why is it never me? I'm not asking to die, but why must I go through all this pain. God, please help me get through this war. Hoping my questions and plea would be answered.

Winston came out of the house, his Thompson pointed to the ground, his finger never leaving the trigger even during a state of no danger. "Okay, Bravo Team let's get to this bridge." With that order, all sixty-nine men stood up and proceeded to the next intersection. Looking down the street where Jose and I ran across, carts and rubble littered the street with a church looking right at me, untouched. Warmth filled my body, my mind informing me that maybe this was God's sign that even amid death and destruction, the strength in God will always stand unharmed.

The bridge was small, only stretched the length of thirty feet, but wide enough to roll a tank over. It was made of limestone, and the water that it stood over was clear with the sky's reflection painted on the water's surface. Cobblestone walls ran away from the bridge on either side only to be met by the creek a few feet away.

*France is so beautiful when the land is not
burnt and destroyed by war.* Looking around the
picturesque area that we had to defend and possibly
destroy.

"I want the two machine guns placed on either
side of the bridge for crossfire. I want teams of
riflemen lined up against the walls as well with twenty
men to be stationed in the houses right behind for
higher elevation fire. We will defend this bridge, boys."
Winston's voice echoed leadership as all of Bravo
Team filled their positions. I placed myself against one
of the walls, three men away from one of our machine
guns. Kneeling so only my rifle and the top half of my
head was visible was the best form of cover that I was
given.

The evening sun's glow splattered the outskirts
of Paris in shadows and colored the water with golds
and oranges. My eyes grew heavy, but the sight that
laid on the other side of the bridge kept me awake
and filled my eyes with beauty. Beyond the street and
houses with trees dotting the intersections stood the
Eiffel Tower. The black silhouette was the highest
building on the horizon. To top all of this, there were
no flashes of artillery in the distance or no crackling of

small arms fire, only the tranquility of birds and leaves rustling in the warm evening air.

Winston came walking down the line tapping random people to go back and switch with the men in the houses for a little rest. "Warren, go to one of the houses and rest for a little. I don't think we will have to fight tonight." His voice was calm and relaxed, helping convince me to replace the stone wall with the inside of a house.

"Thank you...sir." Giving him the respect that I always had for him before standing up and retreating to the house right behind me as men from the house came filing out to patch up the holes that started to form in the line.

The house was empty, no furniture or lamps, only the shelves and ceiling lights interrupted the hollowness of the house. The stairs squeaked after every pressured step and the upstairs rooms matched those of the downstairs. The wooden floors held a film of dust above them and the windows were covered in grime, but thanks to the warm evening we opened them to give us a better view of what was on the other side of the creek.

I sat down as eight other men took their positions on the second or first floor by the windows. In the room that I was stationed was another man taking a position by the window.

"Hello, my name is Warren. And yours?" Shaking his hand while placing my rifle up against the wall holding the window.

"My name is Alex, Alex Fray." Returning my handshake and going back to looking out the window.

He was a short man, possibly five feet and six inches with thick brown hair and dark blue eyes. He was from Philadelphia and worked at his dad's barber shop.

"Do you want to do shifts throughout the night, while the other one gets some sleep?" I asked Alex right after he took a loud yawn.

"Yeah, that sounds fair enough." We both agreed that one of us will catch a few minutes of sleep while the other one looked out the window to make sure we didn't wake up to an attack.

As the evening sun rested behind the horizon so did Alex. My watch was just starting with the rest of Bravo Team looking in the same direction. The night sky's light filtered into Asnières, I looked up in wonder as the number of stars that were visible was incredible.

The water reflected off the moon's light and illuminated the streets and narrow alleyways. In the horizon, the distant glow of war was a reminder that fighting is constant and never ends.

"Hey Alex, it's your watch now." Saying the words gently to not startle the poor man. It felt as though my watch was two hours long with the placement of the moon drastically changed from the beginning of it.

"Okay, I guess no Germans thought it was a good idea to attack at night?" Alex said jokingly, rubbing his eyes and sitting upright, leaning his rifle against the windowsill. I pulled away from the window and placed my rifle against the wall while tilting my helmet a little lower to cover my eyes.

"Wake me up when you want to sleep again." My words rolling off my lips as sleep overcame me and the sight of the dusty floor vanished into a pit of darkness.

"Warren wake up." Alex's voice washed into my dream and pulled me back to reality. My eyes peeled open to reveal the morning light and the commotion of men and trucks.

"Didn't I say to wake me when you wanted to sleep?" Confused on why it was light out and not the dead of night. Standing up and reaching for my rifle, I looked outside and saw a wonderful sight. Tanks and trucks followed by columns of men poured over the bridge towards us, all American soldiers. Talking, laughing, and cheering deafened the air with the mixture of diesel engines and wheels turning.

"Yeah, but I wasn't tired. Paris is liberated by the way. The German garrison surrendered earlier this morning. I don't know where we are being assigned to now, but most likely not Paris." Alex's voice barely coming over the enormous noise of tanks, trucks, and men talking.

"I wish we can see it for a day or two at least." Getting my bearings together while walking downstairs with Alex to regroup with the rest of Bravo Team.

The morning was refreshing and felt as though the war ended, but it was only just the start of the end. The noise was deafening with the constant rumble of M4 Sherman tanks rolling over the bridge and advancing east of Paris to keep pushing the Germans out of France. Trucks full of men and others towing artillery followed behind, with columns of men marching on either side of the traffic. Winston with the help of Captain was standing on a large crate to help direct traffic, both were thrusting their arms in different directions to ensure the best flow of armor and men.

"Lieutenant Jones, where is Gold Company stationed?" Yelling over the volume of vehicles and other men.

"We are by the church. Unfortunately, we won't be staying in Paris! New orders came in, and we need to make a fast approach to the Belgian border by October. If the Allied forces can do this, the war may be over by New Year's!" Winston's voice barely coming through the massive amount of traffic that was surrounding us.

My heart sank a little, not being able to stay in Paris was upsetting, but if this push works then I could celebrate New Year's in Paris, or Berlin, or London if the company was sent home early. But that was in the future, for now, we should make sure everyone is accounted for and start our march to Belgium.

"Sorry that we won't be in Paris for a few days Warren." Alex sympathetically saying to me as we walked towards the church in the town's center. The noise of armored vehicles lowered as we distanced ourselves from the traffic.

"It's okay, I can see Paris another time and the way Lieutenant Jones was talking, we might be able to see Berlin in a few months." My voice quieting with the volume of our surroundings. In response to the silence church bells announcing the time of day and alone piano's voice echoing throughout the alleyways and streets.

Asnières did not look like Lisieux in any way. Except for the layout of the houses and the feel of the cobblestone roads on our feet, but there was a lot that was different. No bodies littered every street and there weren't puddles of blood draining into the sewers. Piles of debris and destroyed houses did not stretch down streets and alleyways. The stench of burning wood mixed with rotting flesh was not sprayed into the air and inflaming our nostrils.

When we reached the church, everyone was lounging around, talking or cleaning their rifles. The source of a beautiful tune coming from a piano was that of Lieutenant Thomas, who nobody knew until now could play piano or any instrument in that case. The tune was soft and made everyone think of the events that already happened. The people they lost, friends that were killed right in front of them, or the towns that we have been in and have seen, destroyed and covered in rubble.

I sat down on a nearby house's steps with Alex next to me, the piano entering my mind and stirring up emotions. *Why must war happen? When will my death be the next that Winston must report about?* Tears formed in my eyes with my head lowered looking at the ground as both my hands gripped my rifle to keep me from falling over.

"Hey, are you okay?" Alex asked me as he noticed a tear dropped from under my helmet onto the light gray stone of the stairs turning it dark. Placing a hand on my opposite shoulder while resting his rifle against the railing of the stairs. "You shouldn't cry here. If Captain comes back and sees you crying, he will send you to a field hospital, and if the others see you crying, then they will see you unfit for battle. Warren, I know this has been hard so far, but you can't break. You are strong and brave, word got spread about how you got your squad away from the sniper."

"Private Taylor died though, so did Lewis, and Jose died right in front of me. These people died because of me, and two of them could still be living if I acted quicker." My voice trembled as the names of dead men poured out. I could feel my throat tighten up and tears about to burst through the dam. "But you're right. I can't cry here, maybe I shouldn't be here at all. Volunteering was a mistake, and I should have listened to my mom that night." Sitting up, I brushed the tears away with my sleeve. Looking at Alex who was staring back at me with a smile, giving me relief and comfort that someone understood that I couldn't take all of this.

"Hey, Lieutenant! Play something uplifting will ya!" Alex's voice yelled as all the men agreed. Thomas stopped the song he was on and started up a new one with higher keys and a faster pace.

"Thank you, Alex. For understanding that is. I know I'm not the only one who wants to cry, but I just can't take the death anymore." The sadness draining from my body as the light-hearted music entered my soul and began to make my feet tap to the rhythm.

"You aren't the only one in this company and definitely not the only one in the allied forces. Death will always be around you, there's no stopping that, but the thing you can stop is how death affects you." Alex's voice was smooth and reassuring. His words were what I needed, and they made clear sense on how to get around this depression.

It was mid-afternoon before Winston and Captain came back to the church. Both went into a house across the street from me where the other officers were talking about the next phase for this company and other companies around us. Looking around from the stone steps I was sitting there were some men who were taking a nap, others talking about home or how this war is going, and the rest including me were cleaning our rifles to make sure they were not going to jam on us during life or death situation. Alex went off inside the church to pray with a few others for the safety of themselves, the safety of this company, and the safety of their families.

Looking around made me realize that Gold Company was short of being at full strength, but we were still an able body fighting force. I could still see the deaths of already so many men who I knew. My mind said that this would be another easy march to another empty town tomorrow, but my gut said that wherever we are about to go will be worse than our night jump into Lisieux. I was ready for the battles to come and my mind was starting to feel the numbness of what war brought. Accepted the feeling of not breaking down after someone was gunned down next to me, but I would still hold those images. The images are what will haunt me, not the fact of someone dying, but that of the scene of friends being killed will never leave my eyes.

"Mail truck!" A voice yelled in a joyful scream, and with that, every man of Gold Company ran towards the truck which held dozens of sacks full of letters and packages in the back. As the truck rolled to a stop in front of the church, men huddled around it, ready for their name to be called for their mail.

I hope mom wrote me a letter. The anticipation of my name being called sent vibrations all over my body, eager to read the words that were placed there by my mother´s pen.

"Johnston!" The man in the back of the truck started rattling off names, one by one he reached in a sack and handed out letters or packages meant for men of Gold.

"Here!" A man behind me said reaching out a hand while his package was being passed back to him.

"Fray!" Alex reached up for this letter while making sure the mail carrier knew of his presence.

"Warren!" My heart paused, and my hand shot up, the thin sliver of an envelope was the best thing than Paris during this war so far.

"Here!" My voice screaming to make sure I received the letter. Joy came to my whole body as the letter started to get passed back in my direction. The white envelope with red and blue lines covering the edges was the first sign I knew it was from my mom as those were the only envelopes she used to mail to family. When the letter was in my reach, I quickly snagged it and ran back to the stairs before the arrival of the truck. The envelope was thin and, on the front, wrote, "Elizabeth Warren 18 Greenhill Rd. Dayton, Iowa."

Sitting on the stairs, I looked at the envelope for a few more seconds making sure it was real. Taking a deep sigh of relief, I opened the letter. The crisp tearing already creating tears inside my eyes. The single piece of paper folded into three sections was the only thing in the envelope.

Dear Joseph,

I miss you greatly, and so does Dale. I have been doing what you asked of me and have been making sure he is nowhere near the evening news, but I have been listening and pray that every battle they talk about didn't involve your company. I worry about you constantly, praying for you every night before I go to

sleep and the church has created a group for families
who have loved ones in the service. The farm hasn't
been easy to maintain, but Mrs. Simpson gave us
some of her farm hands for free. I told them that
money would be small, but a home cooked dinner
would always be prepared for them. I cannot wait for
your return and the places you have seen. Jane's son
came home last week, he is missing a leg and doesn't
seem the same. She said he was part of the invasion
of France and got injured by a landmine during the
beach assault. Please be safe my love, Dale also prays
for your safe return.

> *Your loving mother.*

When my eyes left the words, I could feel warm
streams of tears flowing down my cheeks and onto the
letter creating small wet spots. Wiping the tears away I
folded the letter back up and placed it inside one of
my inner jacket pockets. "*I promise I will come home*
safe." My eyes were scanning the street for any
familiar faces to find out when we will be moving out
tomorrow and caught the sight of Winston, leaning
against a wall of a house looking for the men who
were just sitting around reading the mail or any of the
newspapers that were brought in.

"So, what is this about a push into Belgium?" Breaking his focus on a small group of men who were looking at a copy of a newspaper some guy's mom sent over.

"Huh, oh yeah. Our division is tasked with spearheading the advance into Belgium and stopping at the Luxemburg border. We will have two other companies supporting the advance, but we will be the southernmost one. The push starts in two days when we are brought up to the front lines. If this works, I feel that the war will be over by Christmas." His leaning stance against the stone wall changed into a straighter posture with crossed arms as he talked about the operation. His eyes showed confidence and determination. "We should be able to reach the border before winter comes. The problem is, if we don't, I don't think winter uniforms will come in time."

"Well, that's an even bigger motivation for the men to push through." I cracked a smile and chuckled a little, causing Winston to laugh as well. "So, we are marching to the front lines tomorrow then?" Looking up in curiosity as the sky filled with a low roar. The sound intensified, one by one P-51 fighter planes whizzed by us, low enough to spot the pilots inside, one waving to us as he looked down onto Paris and its suburbs. The planes bodies were extremely bright with the reflection of the sun bouncing off the metal and the bright yellow and blue paint identifying their squadron marked on their tails. Some men jumped up and started cheering, others were yelling and throwing their helmets up in the air.

"Yeah, first thing in the morning." His words trailing off with his attention locked onto the fighters flying above.

After two days of marching, Gold Company reached the front lines. We were placed with other companies that made up our regiment, most of these men I didn't remember, but some seemed vaguely familiar from training. The front line was extremely different than the reserve lines, from the fact that there were thousands of more men and vehicles driving in every direction. Tanks were caked in mud with dents and other blemishes indicating the battles they went through. The men seemed to be ghostly, their eyes showing no life and their faces dirty from the constant grinding of pushing the Germans back. Open bed trucks filled with wounded men driving away from the front off to field hospitals clogged the roads leading away.

Random thundering claps of artillery fire jolted my body, their target miles away and unable to see from our position.

"I'm never going to get used to that," I said out loud trying to speak above the shots while hunkering down under a tarp with Alex and two other privates from Gold. There was a light rain, the type that is annoying and causes the roads to become glue, slowing down any advance we were trying to make.

"Neither am I, but at least this will be the last time next to them. Any other time we hear mortars, it will be incoming." Alex's words weren't comforting. Instead, they made me think. Thinking of our company walking through a forest or a field and not even hearing the firing of the guns, only the screeching of the rounds rushing towards the ground right before the explosion and shower of shrapnel.

"Anyone know what today's date is? I want to write a letter to my sweetheart back home." A young private who sat next to me asked. His face was clean and fresh, unscathed from the horrors of war.

"September third." Alex chimed in before either me or the other private could answer. "I heard that our regiment is being ordered to advance into Belgium tomorrow. I guess there won't be that much resistance,

because of the massive airborne invasion up north."
Finishing before an artillery battery fired off one last
round before ceasing fire till tomorrow.

"Lieutenant Jones told me that our regiment is
tasked with securing the southern part of Belgium,
around the Ardennes. He did say that because the
forest is so dense that resistance there should be
minimal." Telling the men around me, as they all took
interest on how close we were to Germany. "We will
see how this week goes, with the advance starting
tomorrow."

That night was the first I didn't sleep at all,
every attempt to sleep was halted by the rushing
horrors of what has and will happen.

*"Incoming mortar round! Take cover!" Winston
said as we rushed for the safety of anything. The
mortar screaming to the ground, landing right behind
him throwing his body five feet forward. His still face
and burning back indicated he was dead. I couldn't
breathe, my heart was racing out of my chest into my
mouth.*

*"Fall back, there's too many of them!" The voice
telling me to get up and run, but I couldn't, my body
wouldn't let me. Men were being shot in every
direction, bodies falling to the ground, puddles of*

rainwater turning to thick blood, screams from wounded and dying filled the air. When I got out of my cover to make a run for it, I could only take a few steps before I dropped to the ground, my back stinging in multiple areas. Then everything went calm, and darkness filled my eyes.

When I opened my eyes, I was back on the front lines, drenched in a pool of cool sweat. *It was just a dream. All a dream.* The night felt eerie, the light rain of the day turned into a soft mist that covered everything with a thin layer of water. The quietness of it all was the most uncomfortable thing. Being around constant noise for almost five months now can change the appearance of pure silence. Taking a few deep breaths, I laid my head down back on the rolled up wool blanket and closed my eyes.

"Warren wake up, time to go." Winston's voice waking me up from what seemed like a ten-minute nap. The air was cool, and the soft mist that I woke up to now lingered on the grass and everything else. The whole camp seemed to be a rustled bee's nest. Constant movement and noise, which felt more comfortable than the silence of last night.

"Okay, where is Gold being positioned?" I asked standing up and gathering all my equipment while checking my rifle to see if it is in good condition.

"Gold is gathering by the artillery, once we are all gathered. Our task is to capture the town of Bertrix and hold it till the relief column comes. Once they come, we are ordered to quickly advance to Neufchâteau and hold that for the rest of the day. After that, we are tasked to secure a bridge into Luxembourg." Winston filled me in on all the information that was given to him as well. Two towns in three days seem fast paced but stretching out the war isn't any better.

"Alright Gold Company form up here!" Captain's voice coming through all the other noise. Men started rushing over to him eager to advance and fight some more Germans. When Winston and I reached where Captain was standing, he started giving out our task and how he wanted the plan to be executed, "Our task for this big push is to capture and secure the town of Bertrix. Once we do that a relief force will come up and allow us to keep pushing. Intel states that resistance should be light, but take serious measures on this operation, boys. Let´s move out."

The march towards Bertrix was quiet. Our company was supported by Bravo Company and a tank column. I felt as though this force could not be defeated, whether that was the sensation of having eight M4A1 Sherman tanks by our side or the fact that five hundred or so men were marching in unison.

The open fields quickly turned into dense forests, full of dark places for enemy troops to hide and set up an ambush. The low rumble of the tanks turned from a signal of strength to a signal of vulnerability. "*This doesn't feel right.*" Gripping my rifle tighter and placing my finger lightly on the trigger. The tanks were in the lead while all the men walked a few feet behind, everything was silent, and that scared me. My heart was pounding out of my chest, my mind screaming to get to cover now, but my body just kept walking with everyone else.

In the corner of my eye, I saw a quick movement. Then a short flash followed by an explosion as the lead tank burst into flames.

"Ambush!" Captain screamed ducking for cover as two MG42s opened fire sending hundreds of rounds in our direction. Throwing myself into a bush, I could see the lead tank engulfed in flames, the men trying to escape, but were either shot or couldn't survive their burns. Men who could not reach cover in time were ripped apart by the machine guns. Then more explosions as grenades, rockets, and tank rounds went off. *Please God, protect these men and me.* The noise created ringing in my ears, the forest was so dense that the sounds didn't travel.

"Medic! We need a medic over here!" A man on the other side of the road was yelling, holding a bloodied hand of a wounded friend. The tanks started to fan out, destroying any vegetation that laid in their path, trying to create a shield for us to collect our wounded as well as form a plan of attack.

"Stay behind the tanks, don't get caught by the machine guns!" Winston's voice came over the chaos as he started to pull men and ordered them to get any wounded and place them behind the tanks. The tanks fired round after round as their machine guns sprayed the forest in front of them ripping apart bushes and stripping the bark off the trees. Large oaks were snapping, and dirt was being flung fifty feet in every direction from the tank rounds and grenades detonating.

The screams of men being shot while trying to run to a different position added to the chaos. I could hear the voices of German troops yelling as more machine gun fire and explosions continued. I took a few random shots, more scared to be out of cover than fight. Glancing over to my left I saw men covering the road and forest floor, small fires started to form from the constant explosions. There was also a boy hiding behind a rock, no gun in hand but both of his hands covering his ears as tears rolled down his panicked face.

"Cease fire, cease fire!" The crackle of rifles and the ripping of machine guns halted. Only the cries and moans of wounded men, the popping of burning wood and warping metal kept the forest from being silent. The smell of burning wood and diesel created a distasteful scent that clogged the nostrils. There was a thin layer of smoke covering the forest, making the battlefield ever eerier.

With the tanks standing still and smoke pouring out of their barrels, Winston and a few other men went ahead to scan the area making sure it was safe for the column to continue. Looking around to see if anyone needed assistance lead me to another horror. In the group of wounded, I caught the sight of Alex. His body was limp, and a medic stood over him looking down respectfully.

"Is he dead?" I said bluntly rushing over to the medic.

"Yes, got hit too many times. If you excuse me, there are other wounded." The medic left, leaving me and Alex's body alone. I could see it now, the amount of blood soaked into his uniform, the exit holes ripped through his jacket showed that he got hit five times, all in the gut.

"I'm sorry my friend." Lowering my head and saying a prayer, *Lord, please take this man into your arms and protect him from the horrors this war has brought upon. Also, please protect the other men in this group from any further dangers. Amen.* Raising my head, I walked away from the wounded and rejoined the rest of Gold and Bravo companies.

"We will continue this push; the ambush was only a small group of German troops. Bertrix is only an hour away, the tanks will continue the lead while Gold will follow behind them. Bravo took the most casualties, so they will finish the rear. Bertrix shouldn't be heavily defended if at all, so stay alert, but don't get scared. Move it out!" Captain ordered us as we continued our march through the forest to the small town of Bertrix.

As the seven tanks and now four hundred and sixty men kept marching towards Bertrix, the forest became less dense. We kept our guard up, never losing focus of our surroundings. My finger lightly pressed on the trigger, my eyes scanning the forest for any movement, but my heart was racing, and my breathing was quick and shallow.

After the hour of travel, we reached the end of the forest and enter the town of Bertrix. *"Do all towns look the same?"* Looking around and seeing similar housing structures with small gardens scattered around the town, and a small bridge, but big enough for the tanks to get over was the first thing that came into view. It was a gray stone bridge that might have been standing there for hundreds of years.

"Winston, grab twenty men and secure the first street. The tanks and everyone else will wait here." Captain's voice rang out. Winston tapped me on the shoulder while getting the other men for the team.

"Alright let's go." Winston placing his hand in the air and motioning it forward. The team and I rushed over the bridge and pushed on to the first intersection. The place was quiet, white flags or sheets hung outside windows, signs in French and Dutch were placed on either side of the road, "Aucun

Allemands ici."

"Hey Howard, what do those signs say?" A man from Bravo Company asking his friend who I supposed spoke and read French.

"It says that there are no Germans in this town. Lieutenant, I recommend that we send half this team back to tell the column that the town is abandoned while the other half keeps moving forward to see if there are any people in this town. Sir." The man who could read the signs telling Winston, who after a short time of thinking agreed and sent five men from each company back to the column.

"Let's keep moving men. We have to make sure those signs aren't a lie." Winston ordered us, moving forward through the tight streets of Bertrix.

Really hope there's no ambush. All our rifles were up, scanning the windows and alleyways. We were hugging the walls of the houses and running across streets to not be picked off by potential snipers.

We were half inside the town when the roaring of the tank engines came to life. The column was moving forward into the town and securing the first part of our advance to the Luxembourg line. Crossing the last street in Bertrix was a relief knowing that there were no Germans in the town, but something stopped us in our tracks and made Henry throw up his lunch. The smell was horrible, something that I could never forget. Turning the corner around a house was a pile of burnt bodies, still smoldering from the flames.

"What the hell is this? Trying to grip what was in front of me while covering my nose from the smell. I stood frozen, not able to move. Winston and few other guys went up to the bodies to inspect them and try to figure out why they were in a pile burnt.

"I don't know who these people were. The bodies are so burnt that there's no way to identify them." Winston said under a small cloth he carried in one of his coat pockets. Turning around to look on the other side of a house my eyes caught something laying on the ground. I walked over to what seemed to be cloth. Kneeling in front of it and picking the soft white cloth up with my hand solved the mystery of who the people in a pile were.

No this can't be. The Germans couldn't just kill innocent civilians, because of their religion. Turning around so the rest of the team and Winston could hear me, I shouted, "Hey guys! I think I know who these people were." My voice more startled and shaky than I wanted to sound, but if this cloth was the only clue to who these people were, then it was okay for my voice to be that way.

"What did you find Warren?" Winston said walking over to me, but then stopped a few feet in front of me. Seeing the cloth in my hands also helped him understand who these people were.

"Lieutenant, what did Private Warren find? A man from Bravo asked still standing by the charred bodies.

"They're Jews. Warren found a cloth with the star stitched onto it. When the column gets up here, I'm going to speak with the Captains of both companies and see what we should do with this situation. For now, secure this area and wait for the tanks." His voice was still in perfect pitch, but only I could hear the tone in his voice of holding back tears.

Placing the cloth in my pocket, I stood up and gathered with the rest of the team to mark out positions for securing the area. After a few minutes, the tanks and the rest of Bravo and Gold Company joined us at the end of Bertrix. It was only a matter of time till the relief force was to get here so we would be able to keep pushing forward.

When the two Captains reached our position, Winston walked over to them and presented the situation. "Captains, we have a situation." Their faces went to confusion and tense.

"What is it, son?" Captain said looking nervous as if we uncovered a massive German force was coming towards us.

"We found a pile of burnt bodies, sir. But the problem is sir, all of them are Jews." Winston said still trying to hold back the tears that so badly wanted to be released.

"I say that we bury the bodies while we wait for the support force." Bravo Company's Captain said looking over to our Captain who nodded in agreement. "Lieutenant, see to it that these bodies be buried properly."

"Yes, sir." Winston saluted them both and told a group of Privates who were standing by to help bury the bodies.

An hour went by, and the twenty bodies of Jewish civilians were all properly buried. In the same hour, the support force came into town allowing our force to continue pushing forward to our next target. When everything was secured, and our force was ready to move, we did, to our next target.

After a few hours of marching and regaining my composer from finding the horrific sight, Neufchâteau was in sight. Forward scouts informed the

Captains that there was a large German force who were well protected behind sandbags and stone walls waiting for us.

"Best way to do this is charge right in and take them by surprise. I want the tanks to form a screen as Bravo and Gold follow on their tail and take as much ground quickly as possible." Overhearing Captain describe our battle plan while fighting off the incoming winter.

The ground and the village were now covered with a light coating of snow, the first signs of winter. The air now crisp and our fall uniforms starting to lose their usefulness against the incoming winter elements. The smell of gunpowder, burning oil, and burning flesh from explosions polluted the air, mixed with the sight of thick black smoke rising to the heavens.

When the tanks got into position, we wasted no time and started our attack. The line of tanks bursting out of the tree line and our men following right behind did catch the enemy by surprise, but not for long.

"Keep pushing forward! Stay behind the tanks if you have to, but for God's sake push forward!" The orders from Captain was the only motivation to keep moving through a wall of bullets.

The earth shook beneath my feet, as the tanks guns opened fire on the hidden positions and buildings that housed enemy troops. There was no protection, only the backs of the seven remaining tanks. I couldn't show my head, or hundreds of rounds would be coming in my direction. Dirt and snow were being flung all around from tank rounds and grenades.

God, please protect these brave men and me. Right as I finished my prayer, the tank in front of me opened fire, the explosion of the round sprinting out of the barrel created tremendous ringing in my ears. Then a house, which contained two machine gun nests came crashing down. The screams of men being trapped and pinned under the crushing weight didn't put joy into my soul but of fear.

The dust cloud gave pause to the attack only for a few seconds, but those seconds were not as peaceful as I was hoping, it was an eerie silence that scared me thinking I became deaf. Then the machine guns and screams of death came rushing back, filling my ears and filling my stomach with knots.

"Capture that wall!" Captain's words made most of the men who were taking cover behind the tanks take the chance and run forward.

Here it goes. Taking one deep breath, I turned the corner of the lead tank and bolted to the stone wall. Dodging round after round as it felt if every German was aiming at me. The soft powder of the snow resembled that of a peace flag, submerged under the deep red of spilled blood during the war.

A soldier who ran by me dropped to the ground instantly. His body slung to the side as a round entered his body. His helmet flew off with his rifle dropping to the ground. To my left were four of the seven tanks and most of the charging force, the white field being painted with dirt and blood, a blank canvas of winter now being tarnished by the wickedness of war. As my eyes turned to my right a nearby tank burst into flames, men were thrown back from the concussive force, others laid on the ground motionless, and the horror of men screaming while the fire destroyed their bodies slowly. The nightmare of an officer pulling out his pistol to end his life before the fire did will forever be carved into my head and haunt my dreams. But I had to keep pushing unless I wanted to die too.

When I was five feet from the wall, I tossed myself into it. That was the first part of keeping my life, the second part was to survive the town's capture.

I raised my rifle over the wall and took aim at any enemies who came into view. Men of Gold and Bravo filled the wall, releasing round after round into windows, weak cover, and doorways. The release of energy coming out of the rifle barrels brushed off the top layer of snow on the wall revealing the gray of cold stone.

The trigger felt light on my finger as each bullet hit their target, dropping men one by one. As we held the wall, others charged forward rushing into houses and shops. Flashes came from windows, and muffled explosions blew small dust clouds out of open windows and doors. The surviving tanks drove right down the streets, machine guns ripping apart walls and men. Not stopping for anything or anyone, leading to the death of many German soldiers.

After three hours of fighting, house to house shooting, and hand to hand combat, Neufchâteau was finally ours. My face was covered in dirt and someone else's blood. I could not move; my body was so tired. We lost so many men and most of our tanks. Bravo Company was reduced to no more than eighty men, while our company stood with hundred and twenty men still able to fight. We were left with three tanks, but only two still had ammo.

"Now we just need to wait for the support force," I said to Winston who sat next to me on a set of stairs. Both of us were tired and covered in dirt.

"Yeah, the support should come tomorrow morning. Warren, you realize that this town was defended by SS troops, right?" Winston looked at me with a face I have never seen before. His eyes showed sorrow, but everything else showed concern. I noticed on one of the bodies that the SS insignia was on the collar.

"No, I didn't know." My head was now filled with fear. Hitler's SS troops were dangerous and highly feared by every man in the company, if not the Allied forces.

My eyes lowered to the ground playing flashbacks of the fight. *How many SS soldiers did I kill today? Were they the ones that killed the Jews in Bertrix?* Questions mixed with visions of the fighting filled my mind so much that when I looked up, Winston was halfway down the street. The setting sun resting on his back with helmet in one hand and Thompson in the other. He looked as though a battle-hardened soldier ready for the next fight, but I knew he was as broken as I was and just wanted to go home soon.

The next day, Gold Company was ordered to make their way to our next objective which was a ridge about five miles from the bridge that we were tasked with capturing. Overnight the signs of winter finally settled. A fresh coat of snow, four inches high covered the remaining part of our march. I was surprised but also thankful that we didn't encounter any resistance. We reached the ridge by sunset, and all the men started digging out a foxhole.

"Better make this foxhole big enough, or we may be sleeping on each other." Winston jokingly commented as we continued our excavation.

"I'll make sure, so I don't have to worry about you snoring in my ear all night." I joked back while throwing a shovel full of snow and earth over my shoulder.

After an hour or so of digging, our foxhole was finally finished and big enough for both of us to sleep comfortably. It was quiet and peaceful, no signs of war or anything that had to deal with the constant death and destruction. It reminded me of mother and how I haven't had a chance to write to her in a while. I reached for my journal and found a pencil buried in the bottom of my pack. My body started to relax as my hand created the start of the letter.

December 7th, 1944

Dear mom,

It has been a grueling six months, but we have pushed back the Germans from France, and now we are almost pushing them out of Belgium. Last month was the last time I saw fighting. It was a horrible scene, and I will save you from the nightmares I encountered. Captain said that our company isn't tasked with anything except to secure a ridge overlooking the Luxembourg border and then defend a bridge a few miles away. Hopefully, the war will end in the next few weeks, but a part of me doesn't think so. Tell Dale that I love him and will see him soon. Our company was reinforced with new soldiers who haven't seen combat at all, the rest of us have been here since June sixth while the other portion has only seen the battle of Neufchâteau. I love you mother and pray every time for my safe return.

Love always,

Joseph H. Warren

The snow was coming down heavier than last month, my foxhole was only big enough for Winston and me to share. We shared my blanket as his was used as a floor to protect us from the wet, frozen ground, but we were never warm. This place is beautiful during the winter, the peaceful snow being untouched from war or human involvement. The trees hung down from the weight of packed snow. The night sky was sprinkled with so many stars that it looked as if every star turned on its light. There haven't been any German soldiers since we got to this position which added to the peacefulness.

"Winston, do you want to take watch or is it safe for both of us to sleep?" Asking him while placing the letter in my jacket, and fixing the blanket, so both of us had enough. Winston sat across from me with extra socks acting as mittens, his Thompson resting against his shoulder.

"I'll take watch, you get some sleep Warren. I'll wake you up when it's your turn." He was certain that it was safe for both of us to sleep but didn't want to take the chance just in case.

"Okay, good night Winston." I hunkered lower into the foxhole, blanket covering all of me and my rifle resting up against a corner of the hole. My eyes grew heavy with the sight of snow falling and the peaceful night of a Belgian winter.

Chapter VIII

Alone, But Not Forgotten

I thought it was a dream of last month, the setting was the same snow-covered trees and cloud covered sky, the screams and explosions sounded the same ear-piercing tone, but the snow, the softness, and pureness that it had didn't register as a dream, but of reality. At the same moment, a mortar shell went off right next to my foxhole, and the gunfire came through my daze. We were under attack, and most of us had little battle experience.

"They are coming from all directions!"

"We need to fall back to the ridge now!"

"Help! Please help!"

"Mom! Mom!"

I was pinned in my foxhole; my whole company was surrounded by the Germans. I couldn't see them, only the flashes of the barrels, the snow was falling in a steady flow, covering the ground with a peaceful white powder as blood soaked into the innocence, making it horrid. I could hear incoming mortar rounds landing around me. I knew if I got out of my hole I would die, but I felt that helping Captain by gathering what was left of our company and move them to the ridge where we might have a chance of survival would be the best option. Looking around the floor of my foxhole, I tried to grab anything I could to help my cover.

My heart stopped, and my lungs felt as they had gone flat. I collapsed to the ground, my eyes flooding with tears and my mind screaming in horror. Just two feet in front of me was Winston, silent and motionless. I carefully turned his body to face me from its hunched down position. His eyes were wide open, bloodshot and skin a ghostly white. His chest was stained red, and his fingers started to develop frostbite. The deathly look that enveloped over the only person I truly cared for away from home created an ultimate fear that no German could bestow upon me. At that moment I truly felt alone, that not even

God was with me. As I stared into his empty eyes the noises of death and destruction infiltrated my ears and panic surged through my body.

"Wake up! Winston, wake up, please! God please, why him!" My voice being canceled out by the intense battle exploding around me. I grabbed his dog tag and placed it in one of my pockets. *Okay, get yourself together. Winston would want you to live. Think Warren, think!*

Looking around the hole desperately and almost in a panic I saw that Winston had two hand grenades and three smoke ones on his belt, I checked to see if he had any clips left, he didn't, leading me to the split decision to grab my grenades and ready for my move.

I loaded my rifle with my second to last clip and got ready to move. I stood up and started shooting, my rifle screaming out rounds as I blindly shot towards where I knew the enemy was, tears rolling down my face as each pull of the trigger and each bullet exiting my rifle was full of rage and hatred towards my enemies. As I pulled the trigger, and nothing happened, I figured my clip was empty. I grabbed one of the smoke grenades and pulled the pin, waiting a few long seconds for the grenade to light. Then a loud hiss followed by sparks that shot out in every direction as the fuse lit. Throwing it close enough gave me cover for my run to Captain's foxhole and tell him I will gather some men to cover the retreat to the ridge. As the smoke started to billow out of the canister, I jumped out of my hole and sprinted hard as possible to my goal.

Constantly ducking from incoming rounds and mortar shells, I kept running. Screams and cries blared over the sounds of war, men screaming for their mom, boys crying to go home, and the heart piercing sound of German voices getting closer and closer to our position. I was at least twenty yards from Captain's hole when a ferocious sting hit my leg. I dropped to the soft cold snow, I couldn't get up, but I knew I was shot. The pain radiating from my thigh started to flood into other parts of my body, numbness started to cloud my head. I couldn't make it, so I slid into a nearby foxhole where both inhabitants were motionless. They were riddled with bullets; one was still looking up at the sky awaiting his departure to heaven. I placed my hand over his eyes and gently closed them. Suddenly, the sound of gunfire stopped, I was too afraid and too much in pain to peek my head out. I just stayed in the hole motionless, like the two dead men next to me. I heard German troops move in, *we lost, and now they are checking for survivors.* I thought. Cracks of gunfire kept going off here and there, a man screaming in pain suddenly stopped with the parallel sound of a pistol going off. I couldn't move and that saved me as two German troops walked by the hole I was in. I passed out from fear and blood loss, I will never see the innocence of snow ever again.

I woke up where I remembered passing out, twenty yards from where I was running to. I looked at my leg and the cold winter night froze the wound shut, my whole body was numb, but in my mind, that was a good thing to fight through the pain. I gazed around where once my company fought, now is a desolated forest clearing filled with mortar holes, splintered tree limbs, burning tanks and trucks, and men of both sides littered the area. Smoke clouded the morning sky and blackened out the sun's warmth, the stench of burning oil and crisp, charred bodies clogged my nostrils. I grabbed a lonely rifle lying next to me to help support my weight as I got up. I still wanted to get to my captain's hole to check if he survived or at least grab supplies to help me get back to friendly lines.

I limped the gruesome twenty yards that seemed to take away all my energy and when I reached his hole my body collapsed. Not to my surprise, he was dead, his body laid there motionless with a thin layer of frost acting like a glass coffin, pistol still in hand ready to fend off his next attacker. I slid into his hole to find any sorts of food and ammo.

"This guy is a mess; how does he keep anything organized?" I said out loud not afraid as I knew no one was around.

I cleared away some useless papers, his journal, and his shaving gear, but then I saw a picture, it must have been new because there was a letter attached to it. It was a letter from his wife telling him how she misses him greatly, that she finally organized the community garden with the neighborhood wives who have husbands in the war. As I kept reading I saw that he had a child, his name was Thomas, and he just turned four. I then grabbed the picture with the most delicate of care, it was his son and wife sitting on a porch swing smiling, making it appear that they were looking directly at him. My eyes started to fog up as tears made their way down my cheeks. I wiped the tears away as I grabbed my captain's dog tags and the picture. I needed to send this back to his wife, or she will find out by some unknown servicemen with no emotions, saying the same line to other shattered wives or mothers, "Your husband died an honorable man, we are sorry for your loss." This did not sit well in my stomach, I found whatever ammo I could, grabbed a few hand grenades, and saluted my captain one last time.

Peeking over the edge of the hole to make sure my surroundings were still safe, I climbed out and just paused for a second to catch my breath and recollect my head, still wondering why I out of my whole company was the only to survive. There were so many better men and boys who died that shouldn't have, I would trade places with all of them if I could, especially Winston.

The wind was sharp, slicing through my uniform and ripping apart my nose like sandpaper. The snow was not the pure white I woke up to, but black and red from the horrors that unfolded around. The innocence of winter could not be seen until two hundred yards away. The sky not blinded by the carnage of war but piercing through the mid-morning clouds and dashing through the still standing pine trees in the area.

I made my way south in hopes of finding a village that was still in friendly territory. Being by yourself in the forest makes a man think, makes him think too much sometimes. *Is anyone following me? What is my family doing? Does my family know I'm still alive or have one of those servicemen come to my mom's door and take away all hope of my returning?* The forest was quiet, almost tranquility quiet where I could build a cabin and live the rest of my days away from the war, but I knew I had to keep going and find some way of either getting to the front lines or contacting my command station.

The afternoon sun was my only source of warmth as my uniform was still a fall issued one and did little to no protection from the Belgian winter. Still no noise except the crunching of the snow from my boots, that sometimes startled me and made me lay down ready to shoot the nearest enemy. No roads, no game trials, no nothing, I was alone in the forest going God knows where in search for a place that was probably gone depending on how far the German's pushed after they attacked my company.

Looking up from the never-ending whiteness of the ground my feet stopped cold, my heart started to race, and my throat closed. Not even ten feet away from me was a boy, standing there looking directly at me. *Was he friendly? Was he an enemy?* He was short in stature, maybe eight or nine years old. Light blonde hair, and fair white skin. His clothes looked home made from his black knitted scarf to his ripe strawberry red mittens, and his coat was of a stone gray that seemed a little too big for him. I just stood there waiting for the boy to make the first move.

"Amerikaans?" The boy asked looking at me confused, but also a little afraid of what my answer will be.

"Ja." Trying to make my best Dutch impression as I pointed to my patch on my shoulder of the American flag. "Amerikann, friend." I knew little to no Dutch before we went into Belgium.

"Heb je hulp nodig?" The boy asked thinking I knew fluent Dutch.

"I don't know what you're saying, I'm sorry," I told him starting to relax from the calm setting that filled the void.

He walked over to me, understanding that we had a language barrier and reached out his hand. I grabbed his hand and waited for him to take me wherever he wanted. I thought to myself that if a young boy was out in the forest, there must be a village nearby that had food and shelter. He led me down an almost invisible hiking trail that the nearby villagers must use for hunting or leisurely strolls during the quiet spring evenings. The forest started to clear, and a village came into view, it was quiet, almost deserted looking. There was no one walking the cobblestone roads, no dogs barking, or music playing out of a cracked window.

We reached a house that if anyone came by it would think it was abandoned. The windows were shut and boarded up, the chimney was silent, and there were no candles or any sort of lighting warming the inside. He knocked on the door in almost a coded manner, a few seconds came by, and the door opened, everything went black, pain raced through my whole body, my wound must have thawed.

I woke up on a bed, dazed and confused on where I am and if I'm safe. The room was plain, only a dresser and the bed were the only furniture in the room. It was clean, but a thin layer of dust seemed to be covering the ground. The window was shut, and heavy curtains sealed the light from entering. The boy walked into the room I was in and looked inside. He saw that I was up and started bolting from where he came. I heard him talking to someone, and then multiple pairs of feet started to flood the quietness that once roamed the hallway and the room I was recovering in. The same man that I saw before I fainted came around the doorway and started looking at me, the boy was right behind him with the exact same ponderous expression of what happens now.

"I am American, I need to know where the American's are. Can you please help me?" The words flew out of my mouth in almost desperation. I guess my face showed concern and fear, because of not knowing if the man would hand me over to the Germans, but the way he walked towards me and how he cared for the boy made me relax and understand that he was the father of the boy. He started walking over to me slowly. He bent down in front of the bed, and paused for a few seconds, possibly thinking of what to say, or what to do with an American soldier. His face hard and emotionless, the mustache was black and bushy with his hair being of the same color and volume.

"You...are...safe here." The man said in broken English, but still understandable. He indicated to me to show him my wound, I peeled the blanket off my body and presented my leg. The wound was tended to during the time I was out. The hole was stitched and bandaged, my leg did not feel numb or in agonizing pain, but an annoying feeling when the blood rushes back from a muscle falling asleep. "I took bullet out, no broken bones." The man told me as he put the blanket over me again.

"Thank you. when can I leave, I must get back to friendly lines as soon as possible before the German's make more of a push?" I asked him concerned attempting to sit up, but my body was so sore from the travel and the battle before that my muscles could not hold up my own weight.

"Rest...be strong before leave. German's not...uh...capture Americans. German's kill Americans, uh...on sight." The man told me now standing up and walking towards the door where the boy was still standing studying me until he could draw a clear image in his head.

A few days went by, and I felt confident enough to leave my caretakers. I got my uniform on, tightened all the straps, cleaned my rifle and checked how much ammo I still had. When I went downstairs both the man and the boy were there waiting for my departure. I shook the man's hand and rubbed the boy's hair. He looked up at me and smiled, gave me a hug and in return I reached into one of my side

pockets and took out a chocolate bar. The man told
me that the American's seemed to have been pushed
back heavily towards the French border but may have
halted the enemy's advance. He gave me a map as
well as a few freshly baked biscuits to help me on my
journey.

"Dank je," I said to them in respect for what
they did for me. I opened the door and started my
journey back to safety. Winter was still in full force,
and the clouds seemed like an endless blanket
covering all of Europe. The wind was ice against my
cheeks, there was a light snowfall that hung around all
morning. It reminded me of when there was no war,
no death, no horror, only peace. The memories of
where I would be helping mom tend to the fireplace
and play out in the field with Dale who would always
think that being a little brother meant he would always
get first try at sledding down the hill covered in fresh
snow played in my mind.

It was mid-afternoon when I finally stopped to
rest. I sat down behind a large rock and a conifer tree
resting against it giving me some sort of protection
from the falling snow that was still lingering.

I shouldn't be that far from any village, but then again, I haven't heard or seen any German's so who knows how far I must go. Maybe all the way back to Paris. There's a stream about a mile west of where I am if I follow that maybe I can find another village and gather some more food and information. I thought to myself as I sat against the rock, taking one of the biscuits the man gave me before I left out of my pocket. The soft flakiness of it eased all my worries and brought back memories of when mom would make her biscuits with her famous chicken soup.

The memories vanished as a low roaring sound flooded and intensified the area around me. It was coming from behind my position, I quickly grabbed my rifle and got ready for whatever was coming to my direction. I stayed low behind the rock, only the top part of my head was peaking above to see what was approaching. The low roaring sound was a transport truck, driving down the almost invisible road. It was German, but I didn't see any troops sitting in the back at first, but then saw the red cross with a white circle surrounding it.

It's a med truck, that means there is resistance close by, or better yet the front line!

The feeling of being close to safety drowned any negativity out of my mind and heart. A smile came to me, the first time in a long time I showed joy. I stayed hidden till the truck passed, I saw that in the back there were a handful of bodies lying on stretchers and two others sitting hunched over, one with a bandaged wrapped around his head with a red blob closer to where his eye would be. As the truck drove out of sight I made my move, I had clear intentions on where to go now and an even better feeling that I may get out of this alive.

I walked close to two miles, nothing surrounded me except trees, bushes, and more trees. The road that started to vanish from the snow was my only guide to salvation. I threw myself into the closest bush after the quick burst of gunfire rang through the silence of the forest. I didn't see anyone, nor did I see where the gunfire came from, but I didn't hear it again. I waited in the brush for a little longer waiting for anyone to reveal themselves, but no one did. I stood up and resumed my journey, only now was I on edge and checking my surroundings more closely.

The sky was not cloud covered anymore, no snow fell, no sounds either other than the crunching my boots made in the snow. Everything seemed dead that I was the only creature alive in the forest. This sent a hollow feeling surging through my whole body, feeling this alone can damage a person's moral and thought process.

Maybe there is no front line. Maybe the Germans brought back every soldier from the East and made a massive counter attack to repel us, to make us surrender and leave Europe and the world to them. I may never see mom again or Dale, I may never see home again, grow old, find a beautiful girl and raise children. All these thoughts raced through my mind. I knew I had to stop this flood of negativity, put my mind back at ease and finish this journey.

I just kept walking, aimlessly, but not hopelessly. Then I tripped over something, I picked myself up and turned around to see what it was. It was a human leg, frozen to the core, stiff and black. I walked over to it slowly, I took a guess where the face would be and started brushing the snow away. A face came through frozen in a state of sadness, and so did the unmistakable shape of a U.S. Army helmet. I jumped back and then realized there were three other bodies next to this one, all in a single line.

The man was right, they are just executing us and not letting us try to survive in a POW camp. This is barbaric, inhuman, uncivilized, this even goes against the Geneva convention! I just couldn't believe any of this, I couldn't believe they would throw us into a line and shoot us down. Rage ran through my blood, my heart started to race, my mind was still clear though. Get home, but now it was, get home and kill any enemies who cross my path.

I grabbed all four dog tags and placed them in my pocket where Winston and Captain's were as well. I stood straight up and gave one final salute to my fellow soldiers. I continued my trek through this now seemingly endless forest to whatever safety I could find. I reached into my larger back pocket and pulled out the last biscuit I had. It was not as warm and flaky as the first one I ate, but cold and dry, none the less I still ate it as there was nothing else to end my hunger.

Nightfall was shortly coming, and I had to find shelter from the elements and hide from the enemy. *Nothing but these damn trees and bushes all around me. Guess I just have to dig then.* I said to myself as I slipped my shovel out of its holder. I started to dig into the almost frozen ground. It was complete nightfall when I finished my hole, I took everything off and grabbed my blanket out of my bag. *Maybe this will be my grave.* I thought to myself as I pictured a German coming up to my hole and emptying a whole magazine into my sleeping body. It's been almost a week since I was with my company and almost two days since the boy and the man helped tend to my wound. I closed my eyes and accepted whatever fate was dealt to me, drowsiness came over me, and soon enough I passed out.

Chapter IX

The Journey Home

It must have been pre-dawn when I was jolted awake by the sounds of mortars and small arms fire.

That sounds close! I told myself startled, I felt nervous and hopeful at the same time. Will this be like the night I lost my company, or will this be the opposite?

I shot up, rifle and helmet in hands. I quickly placed my helmet on my head and checked my ammo in my rifle, it was full. I bolted across the snow-covered forest, all these days the forest was my prison, my isolation from the horrid world that lay beyond, but now that door was opened, and war invaded my peace. I was ready for what came before me, death or life I did not mind. I only thought of the men who were fighting for their lives, fighting for their survival, then I thought of my captain and Winston. Those men died in battle, and I could not save them, but these men I could, maybe not all, but some. The forest started to clear, and the battle entered my soul.

This was not a dream, the snow did not seem innocent anymore, but guilty of seeing what man can do upon one another. Smoke choked out the now rising morning sun, burning oil and flesh infiltrated my nostrils and reminded me of what war could destroy. Explosions rocked the ground beneath my feet, and ruined buildings surrounded me. There was a pile of bricks half covered in snow with a sign laying on top still trying to indicate what village this is or was.

Bastogne. That name leeched into my mind and carved into my skull. I felt that this battle would not be forgotten, that this isn't just a pocket of resistance, but the last hope of rescuing all of Europe. I tried my best to run down the cobblestone road that paved the way to my mission. No building seemed untouched from war. Hopefully, the civilians escaped before this bloodshed.

The small arms fire started to intensify and screams of pain and commands echoed the hollow street I was on. Nerves were shooting rapidly, my heart was racing a mile a second, this was the second-time urban battles came into my life and the first time was a vivid hellish nightmare that would never leave my mind. The screams and intense gunfire, the hand to hand combat in every building, I never wanted to experience that again. My rifle was tightly gripped in my hands, my eyes scanning the area ready to pounce on any enemies foolish enough to run out of cover. My feet stopped, the sound of running came through my ears, indicating that I was no longer alone, either friendly or enemy troops were moving into my area, I tensed and braced for whoever came towards me. Three bodies came past the corner and laid down behind a mound of debris setting up a plan of attack for any enemy that came into view. I raised my rifle and slowly placed my finger on the trigger ready to take three lives. My breathing took a pause, my eyes grew wide, and my finger released from the trigger and went back to the smooth wood of the stock. I recognized the olive drab color of American uniforms and the dullness of the helmets.

They were Americans, finally friendlies, I can relax a bit, but how do I tell them without startling them and shooting me down? This question raced through my mind then it came to me, *I'll yell my company's name to inform friendlies that reinforcements have arrived.* "Gold company move to secure this area!" I yelled out loud to the world. My legs moved on command, and my body started moving towards the three men.

They turned around and looked at me in confusion, wondering where the rest of the supposed Gold Company was, only to see a weak, dirty body of one soldier running towards them.

"Where the hell is the rest of your company?" One of the men questioned me as I threw my body on the rubble mound.

"I am the only one still alive. I needed a way to acknowledge my approach without you guys shooting me dead." I explained to them catching my breath not out of exhaustion, but out of relief that I was not alone anymore.

"Well my name is Sargent Stevens, next to me is Lieutenant Jamison, and over there is Private O'Malley." Stevens introduced all three of them. His dark blonde hair showing itself under his helmet, his navy-blue eyes connecting with mine. "And welcome to Hell, or previously known as Bastogne. Our forces are trapped, and there is no sign of relief coming, we are running low on ammo and medical supplies. We were able to hold off the German's for two days now, but it doesn't seem like we will be able to survive another two." Stevens informed me as my eyes peaked over the rubble pile to check if the enemy was advancing.

"We also don't have that many men left to hold all sides of the village as well." O'Malley chimed in with a hollow look on his pale face making his red hair stand out more. His steel gray eyes and the other two men held the same emptiness that only came with the overwhelming horror that was war.

"Lieutenant Jamison, what is the plan of attack?" I asked ready for revenge.

"Our objective is to reach the bell tower and spot the enemy positions, so we can inform our commanding officer were to build up the defenses. Our secondary objective is to repel any scouting parties that the enemy puts into this section of the town." The Lieutenant stated, taking out a map of the village and showing me where the forces were as well as what parts of the village were of no importance to either side.

Lt. Jamison peaked his head over the rubble and scanned the area for any movement. I figured his hair was a clean cut from not seeing any under his helmet and his brown eyes were more of a chocolate hazel. I could also see the battle took a toll on him as fresh cuts and bruises covered his face, leaving nothing, but a war-torn soldier who just wanted to go home alive.

"On my mark, we make our way to that house over there." He ordered pointing to a house that took a direct hit from an artillery shell. The roof was caved in, but the front wall was still intact giving us good cover in case of enemy contact. "Ready...now! Move." We bolted to the house, not turning or looking around, our boots thundering down the road making the noise as though a whole company was charging. Sgt. Stevens was the first one to reach the front door and busted through it, O'Malley followed suit, and I with the Lieutenant brought up the rear to cover our entrance.

The house was empty, dark, and dusty. The occupants must have evacuated weeks ago, and only carried what was dear to them. We all sat down for a second or two to catch our breath.

"O'Malley and the new guy go check the second floor just to make sure we don't have any German's waiting for us. By the way, what is your name?" Lt. Jamison said looking in my direction.

"Private Warren, sir. Gold Company, 528th Battalion, 2nd Regiment." I replied, feeling like I was back in boot camp, yelling out my outfit for memorization.

"Okay, Private O'Malley and Warren go inspect the upstairs, the Sargent and I will stay here to watch the road," Jamison told us.

I took point as O'Malley was right behind me going up the stairs. If there were any German's up there, they would already be aiming at the doorway ready to riddle us with bullets. My heartbeat was quickening every stair I passed, I kept my rifle on my shoulder just in case I turned the corner, and there were enemies up there. I stopped at the doorway that was on my left, the light pouring into the landing area before the door. I turned around and looked at O'Malley, our eyes showing the same tension, but we both knew what had to happen. My mouth moving to the tiny whisper of three...two...one. I spun the corner and put my rifle up, so I could look down the sights. The room was emptier than downstairs, it seemed to be a child's room before the people left. *Hopefully, that child is still alive and healthy.* We both went downstairs to inform Lt. Jamison that the upstairs was all clear.

"We will stay here the night, Warren, you will take the first watch and then O'Malley." Jamison gave us the order and sat down on one of the wooden chairs that still roamed the empty space. As night infiltrated the house and drowned the evening light from the street, I took my position by one of the windows. I could hear enemy artillery pounding the other side of the village as the sky flashed white and orange, comfort swelled inside of me, the knowledge that I had others around me, all willing to protect each other, which, erased the broken nerves and splintered anxiety. The sound of small arms fire was too soft to indicate any fights close by and no screams of either German or English also hinted that we were the only souls in the area. I imagined the village before the war, joyful people strolling down the streets, some talking to neighbors, children running and laughing, and farmers tending to their fields.

"Hey Warren, you can get some sleep, I'll take watch now. We will wake you when it's time to move."

Sgt. Stevens said startling me from my daydream.

"Thank you, I need a full night's sleep from all that has gone on," I told him standing up from the window ledge, grabbing my helmet as well.

"Once this battle is over, and we make it out alive I will tell the Lieutenant to send you back behind the front lines. Maybe they will send you home with a medal or two." Stevens replied replacing the space I was at.

The thought of medals and honor never came to my mind. I could only think of the men that died before they had the chance to defend themselves. I thought of Winston's dead frozen body and the Captain's kid who will never see his father or his wife who will never be able to see her husband ever again. That was my true mission, to survive and give these people the comfort and closure they needed, not by a stranger, but by someone who knew the person who perished. I never thought of the positives that came out of this nightmare unless surviving this was a positive. I laid down on the floor with my blanket as the only protection from the cold winter night and my helmet as my only source of a pillow. My eyes became heavy and accepted the long sleep that my body demanded.

"Warren...hey...Warren, wake up we need to move now." Lt. Jamison shook me awake, I opened my eyes and stood up. I grabbed my rifle and helmet and prepared to move towards the bell tower. "Stevens take point; O'Malley take the rear. The bell tower should be two blocks down from us. Hopefully, we get there without any incident." Jamison ordered as we exited the building in our given positions and started walking with caution towards our objective.

The village was eerily quiet, no distance gunfire, no rumbling engines of vehicles, not even the talking of birds. The sky was clear, and the sun gave little to no warmth from the freezing temperatures. We were in a single file line walking down a sidewalk to hug the nearest wall in case of gunfire, our footprints the only indication of life on this side of the village. Stevens raised a fist in the air telling the rest of the squad to halt.

Stevens turned around and whispered, "No enemy contact, bell tower across the street, possible sniper I'm thinking, but hopefully not. Lieutenant, we move on your signal, sir."

"There shouldn't be a sniper in this area, but we will move with caution just in case. Warren, you go first and run towards that door over there. Stevens you will follow, after that, will be O'Malley, and then myself will cover the rear. Understood?" The Lieutenant spoke in almost an uncertain tone. We all understood, and I got ready to run across the open street to a front door that was pressed into the house given some sort of cover.

You will be fine, there's no sniper. Just run, and all will be right. Attempting to calm myself, I looked back to the others and nodded I was ready. I ran to the door; my body was not keeping up with my feet leaving me being thrown against the door. If there was a sniper, he either didn't see me or couldn't get a clear shot. Next was Stevens, just like me, he ran hard and got to the door safely. Both of us were breathing heavily as we waited for O'Malley to run across and join us. He must have been a track star before joining the war because, by the time he started running, he was already pressed against the door with us. Jamison had a clear nervous face, he didn't want to run, but he knew he had too. Jamison looked down took a deep breath and started running, his face now in a panic. He ran into the door harder than all of us, releasing a loud breath of relief, looking at me as if I was confused, which I was a little.

"I lost my best friend to a sniper; the bullet went clean through his skull. Never saw it coming, neither did anyone else." Jamison told me, I could relate, both our friends died before they knew it was their time. "Okay, now onto the bell tower boys." His mood changed and so did his face as if all the dangers couldn't touch us now.

We made our way to the bell tower, it was gray and tan in color from the stones that created it. Snow hung to the sides of the base, and the roof seemed to be scrapped by an artillery round early on. We got inside and headed towards the stairs. The dust clung to everything and the mildew stench mixed with almost a mothball-like scent engulfed the air in the tower. The steps were creaky and made me worry if the sound would notify anyone upstairs. We got to the third floor when we realized there was a sniper in the tower, but he was already dead. O'Malley went over to the German's body and turned him over.

"Died of hypothermia" O'Malley stated letting go of the once German sniper and letting him continue his endless sleep.

"Well, now we know we're alone again," I commented as I signaled to take point to reach the top of the tower.

We reached the top with ease; the sight would have been breathtaking if there weren't any dark smoke clouds billowing towards the sky or if the buildings were not destroyed and collapsed. Stevens and Jamison took positions to scan the surrounding area for enemy movement, O'Malley and I secured the door to protect our backs.

"Looks like we will have company soon," Stevens said in almost a scared tone looking towards Jamison.

"What do you see, Sargent?" I asked concerned myself.

"Looks like fifty German infantry and two Tiger tanks. All of them coming towards us." Stevens said getting up from his position and walking towards the door.

"Our orders were to get to the bell tower and repel any scouting parties, not to repel anything larger than that! Especially a force with two Tiger tanks." O'Malley barked, obviously scared out of his wit.

I too was scared, fifty men was already too many enemies for a group of four to hold off but adding two unstoppable beasts like the Tiger tank into the scene and well, death was certain. We all looked at

Jamison waiting for our orders, I knew that none of us wanted to fight, but we all also knew that if they got passed the rest of the American force would fold and surrender.

"We have to fight, I know it's not logical and highly suicidal, but if we don't stop this force, then they will swing around and hit our forces from behind. If we can take out the infantry first, then possibly we can take out the tanks with less of a difficulty then. We all split up, taking different buildings and start wearing down the infantry. All of us have grenades and enough ammo, save one grenade each for the tanks if you can. Good luck, it was a pleasure serving with all of you." Jamison finished his battle plan with a confidence running throughout his voice. He gave me one last look, a serious look that made me think if he was trying to remember my face in case this was the last time we would see each other.

Everyone shook hands and checked rifles, I saw O'Malley's hands were shaking, and I came over to comfort him, "Hey, you will be okay. We will all make it out of this alive...I promise." He looked up at me and thanked me with a hug.

"Alright boys, let's give them Hell." Lieutenant Jamison said as we all ran out of the bell tower and went our own separate directions to different houses.

Jamison took the house closest to where the enemy would approach from, Stevens took three houses down and across from him. I saw O'Malley run into a house parallel to mine, I was on the second floor of a house that was well-taken care for by its owners. All the furniture was still there, no clutter, and the most shocking thing was that it was unscathed from the surrounding battle. The room I was in used to be the master bedroom, it was large and held a lot of different furniture items. I slowly opened the window to give me a clear sight of the street below perfectly, I placed my rifle on the windowsill for better stability.

The loud rumble of the tanks deafened any other noise, picture frames in the room started to rattle, and a few fell off their stand. I prepared myself for the battle, my hands gripped my rifle even harder as the first few Germans poured into the street, more and more crowded the street, I waited for Jamison to initiate the battle. I fixed my sights on a single German and followed his movement. Suddenly the crackle of gunfire went off, Jamison started the battle. I pulled my trigger, and the German fell to the ground limp. O'Malley's window flashed as he too was firing into the enemy below. My rifle was firing out rounds quicker than I was thinking, I locked onto a German running for cover and saw him drop from the bullet that left my gun. A high-pitched ding noise notified me that my clip was empty, and I had to reload. I pressed the new clip into my rifle and got ready to continue firing. Twenty or so bodies littered the street, blood turning the snow red.

The tanks turned the corner and entered the ambush, their turrets lining up for their shot into any house they thought the enemy was. One of them lining up to pump a round into the house right next to O'Malley's. The thundering sound as the gun opened fire was deafening. A large cloud of smoke and dust filled the street, the front of the house was gone, and a part of O'Malley's had collapsed as well. The other tank took a shot at an empty house between Stevens and my positions. The tanks then started opening fire with their machine guns. Rounds ricocheted off the wall of my house forcing me to duck down. I was still calm, but now on edge, hoping that one of those tanks doesn't take a direct shot at my house.

I got up and sighted on another German, I pulled the trigger, and he dropped. Fear went through my body like electricity. Two Germans busted through the door of O'Malley's house and entered. I wanted to scream his name and tell him to turn around, I wanted to leave my position and help him. I just kept firing, emptying another two clips. When I fired my second to last clip I saw flashes across the street, I couldn't tell if O'Malley was surviving or if he turned around to face his death. The flashes stopped, and no one came out of the house.

By this time, the German force started to pull back, most of the houses around me were damaged from the tanks shells. I didn't let up though, any enemies I saw my rifle stopped them. The street was red and covered in bodies, no pure snow laid untouched. I turned around and slid against the wall, my breathing was fast and heavy. I closed my eyes to try and calm myself, slowing down my breaths and letting go of my rifle. I wanted to break down, I wanted to fill my helmet with tears of pain and frustration. Honestly, I just wanted to go home and away from the war.

"Warren you're still alive!" The voice sounded like Jamison's, but more deep and worried.

"Yeah! I'm still here." I replied letting the Lieutenant know I was still alive. I got up and put my head out the window.

"Stevens is okay, got grazed by one of those machine gun rounds, but he will live. I'm going to check on O'Malley now. You should come down and check for any survivors." Jamison notified me on the rest of the squad.

I picked up my rifle, put my helmet on, and shook the emotions off. When I got outside I wanted to go into the house O'Malley was in to check if he was still alive. I walked over to the door, carefully placing my steps in between the corpses that littered the ground and the puddles of blood that started to form. The door creaked open, and all was silent, I slowly made my way up the stairs to the second floor when I was stopped by Lt. Jamison walking out of the room O'Malley was in. His head down and face red from constant crying.

He can't be dead; he should have been able to get them both if they were making so much noise inside before reaching him. I pondered to myself as Jamison passed me on the stairs as if I were a ghost. When I got to the room, I saw what had happened. Both Germans were dead by the doorway, but

O'Malley was also dead lying next to a nightstand, bullet holes in his stomach and arms. *I'm sorry...I could have saved you, I could have...* The thought stopped as I was interrupted by Stevens running up the stairs to see for himself.

"He was only nineteen. He told me that when the war was over, he was going to take over his dad's watch shop and marry his sweetheart." Stevens said out loud as he knelt by O'Malley putting a hand on his shoulder. "We have to get back to the rest of our men, tell them that we repelled a flank attack and inform them that there may be more like that later."

I agreed, and we both got up and went outside to meet Jamison checking the bodies for intel and possible survivors. We all went through a lot, but our defense may have saved countless more lives.

"We are going the way we came from. Grab any ammo you need and get ready to move. I have O'Malley's tags, and when this is all over, we will come back out and retrieve his body." Jamison said getting up and placing a Luger into his pocket.

"You know if we get caught they will kill you on the spot for having that Lieutenant," Stevens commented pointing to the handgun now securely inside Jamison's pocket.

"That's if we get caught Sargent, which won't happen on my watch." Jamison defended his action. "Let's move out before it gets too dark."

We made it back to the spot where I first encountered these fine gentlemen. Just being with them for only a day seemed so short compared to how I grew on them. We were brothers, we were willing to sacrifice ourselves for the lives of each other. All three of us understood that O'Malley didn't die without a fight and to protect the rest of us from death.

When darkness started to creep into the streets, we stopped for rest at a desolated bakery. The windows were smashed, and nothing was there to eat, there was bread lying around, but the rats and winter already mutilated them. I took comfort on a wooden chair, rifle leaning on the wall next to me and helmet on my knee. Jamison did the same but towards the back of the bakery and Stevens took watch by sitting on a tabletop by the window looking out into the abyss. I closed my eyes hoping that tomorrow will be the last day I should fight. I pressed my head against my left shoulder and fell asleep.

I was thrown from my seat by who looked like Stevens from my hazy morning eyes. Gunfire was erupting, and Jamison was firing out the window towards across the street where there was a German scout party taking cover behind the wall of the house.

"Warren get up and move, there's a back entrance where we will leave from. Once you get out go right down the alleyway and just keep running down that street, you will make your way to our defenses. Go! Now!" Jamison ordered as I jumped up and ran out the building towards the ally way.

"Warren this way!" Stevens shouted further down the alley shooting around the corner.

My mind was in a haze, this had to be a dream, but this is war, and anything can happen. I wanted to stay and fight, but orders were orders, and I had to follow them. I started running towards Stevens and hugging the wall when I reached him.

"Why does Lieutenant Jamison want me to run back to the base instead of fighting?" I asked Stevens over the intense sound of rifle and machine gun fire.

"He told me last night that we have to protect you no matter the cost. You've gone through so much and have helped us complete our mission. If you can get back to the defenses and tell our commanding officer, then our mission was a success, and you will be able to go home." Stevens explained to me in between firing his rifle towards the enemies across the street.

"I want to stay and fight, I can't leave you guys. Yes, I've been through a lot, but that's no excuse for me to leave you two behind." I argued but knew that there was no choice. They wanted me to go, and I knew that if I did stay there would be the possibility of all three of us dying. "Alright, I'll go, but don't die."

"I'll try not to." Sargent Stevens told me as he turned the corner and brought down a German running to the other side of the street. "I will provide cover fire as you run down the street. Just keep running, don't look back no matter what." "Covering fire!" As his rifle screamed alive, his finger pulling the trigger faster than I ever could. I started running down the street, that is when I realized my rifle and helmet were still in the bakery.

Don't go back, no matter what. Stevens voice echoing in my mind as I kept running down the street.

My body was running away, but my mind was screaming for me to turn around and help them. At that moment, my mind took over, and I stopped running. I dove to a nearby stone staircase for cover and to view the battle that was raging on. As my head peeked over the stone railing and my eyes could see the bakery in shambles, the bodies of Germans lying on the road face down in the snow, and the flashes of the guns exchanging bullets at one another. I started to stand up to make my way down the road back to the bakery to grab my rifle and help my brothers, but my move was canceled by an intense explosion that rocked me off my feet and blew dust and smoke into the road covering the view of what was in front of me.

The dust and smoke settled, German voices echoed through the street and bodies started running across to the bakery. My ears were ringing, and it seemed everything was in slow motion. Breathing was hard, and my eyes were in a blur, I tried to regain my focus on the situation, but it was nearly impossible to.

"Let me go! I will pull the pin! So help me God, I will pull this pin!" A voice came through that sounded somewhat like Lt. Jamison's.

I saw two Germans coming out of the bakery dragging a man who was squirming and fighting to break free with a grenade in one hand. The two men threw Jamison to the ground as he landed on his knees, another German came over and pulled a pistol out of his holster. Without hesitation, the man pulled the trigger, and Jamison's body dropped to the snow. I couldn't move, I couldn't do anything. My whole body froze, and my mind went blank. Fear struck my core and did more to my body and mind than the bullet that ripped through the flesh in my leg weeks ago.

Before I could regain control of my body, two gunshots pierced my ears, and the two Germans that pulled Jamison to his death now faced their own as their bodies dropped to the ground. Sgt. Stevens came out of the bakery firing erratically to the enemy. Quicker gunshots silenced the screaming of Steven's rifle as the Sergeant tilted back. His body now falling to the snow next to Jamison's. A German came over to Steven's body and aimed the pistol at his head releasing the bullet from the gun and sending it into the skull of an already dead man.

I have to go now; I shouldn't have turned back, I told myself, standing up and bolting down the street, what I should have kept doing in the first place.

The air was thin and cold, cutting through my face and making my eyes water even more. The slow snowfall brought me back to better, happier times where there was no war, no blood spilled, no friends and brothers lost. The running seemed to be never-ending, passing block after block of ruined houses and shops. Piles of rubble were the new monuments that would be reminders of what hell this village saw.

There it is! Finally, this can end. My voice sounded more cheerful than it should have been as the sandbags and the familiar uniforms of U.S. soldiers came into view.

My legs started to give out, and my eyes could not hold back the tears of released stress. I was nearly two blocks away from our defenses when my legs fully gave way, and I collapsed on the snow-covered cobblestone road.

"Who goes there?" A voice said. I took no notice to who said it as I only could think of the constant feeling of being alone vanishing.

"Private Joseph H. Warren, Gold Company, 528th Battalion, 2nd Regiment." My voice shakily said as tears started running down my face and my breathing quickened. I could not move at all, I just stayed motionless on my hands and knees.

I looked up, and through my tears, I saw two soldiers running towards me. One knelt next to me looking down the road from where I came, rifle on his shoulder ready for any enemies daring enough to come into sight.

"Are you okay?" The first man asked me, bending down, scanning my body for injuries. My mouth could not open, and my voice went silent.

"Medic, we need a stretcher!" The other one demanded, kneeling next to me, his hand on my shoulder. The first sign of safety in a while.

"You will be okay, son." The soothing voice rushed over me as I felt my body being placed on the stretcher. My eyes grew heavy and my body still in a frozen state. Darkness overcame my vision, and the pure snowfall vanished from my sight. The faces of Winston, Captain, Alex, Bryce, O'Malley, Stevens, and Jamison replaced the darkness in my mind. The people I will never see again, only names carved on stone placed in a clean row surrounded by thousands more like them who fought bravely and honorably, but only these will be close to my heart.

Visions of home rushed into my mind then after. Dale brushing the horses and my mother making her sweet apple pie. The illusions felt so real as if I was back home safe and sound. My mother running over to me, hugging me and kissing my cheek. Dale throwing the brush down, running to give me a hug as well. Looking directly at my mom and before the vision faded away, I said one final line.

"Like I promised, I will come home alive."